Emma-Jean Lazarus Fell Out of a Tree

by Lauren Tarshis

SCHOLASTIC INC.
New York Toronto London Auckland Sydney
Mexico City New Delhi Hong Kong Buenos Aires

ISBN-13: 978-0-545-14250-2
ISBN-10: 0-545-14250-4

12 11 10 9 8 7 6 5 4 3 2   9 10 11 12 13 14/0

Printed in the U.S.A.   40

First Scholastic printing, February 2009

Designed by Teresa Kietlinski Dikun
Text set in Mrs. Eaves

To my mom and dad

To David

To Leo, Jeremy, Dylan, and Valerie

With love

Chapter 1

Emma-Jean Lazarus knew very well that a few of the seventh-grade girls at William Gladstone Middle School were criers. They cried if they got a 67 on an algebra test or if they dropped their retainer into the trash in the cafeteria. They cried if their clay mug exploded in the kiln and when they couldn't finish the mile in gym. Two even cried in science, when Mr. Petrowski announced it was time to dissect a sheep's eyeball. Of course Emma-Jean had no intention of participating in such a barbaric and unhygienic activity. But crying was not a logical way to express one's opposition to the seventh-grade science curriculum. Emma-Jean submitted a memo to Mr.

Petrowski, detailing her objections to the dissection point by point. He had excused her from the project.

Colleen Pomerantz was not one of the criers. Which was why Emma-Jean was so surprised when, on a cold February afternoon, she walked into the girls' room and discovered Colleen leaning over the sink with tears pouring down her face.

Emma-Jean's first thought was that Colleen had been injured. The halls of William Gladstone were crowded and hectic. It was possible that Colleen had been struck in the head by a carelessly slung backpack, or accidentally elbowed in the eye by a rambunctious seventh-grade boy.

Emma-Jean approached Colleen, ready to administer basic first aid if necessary.

"Are you hurt?" Emma-Jean asked.

Colleen shook her head and said in a loud voice, "Oh no! I'm really fine." She straightened her body and smiled.

Emma-Jean peered into Colleen's freckled face. She saw no blood or bruising or swelling. Colleen's pupils appeared normal. But even so, Emma-Jean was quite sure that Colleen was not fine. Certainly Colleen was not *really* fine. Emma-Jean spent much of her time observing people, trying to understand them better. Really fine people did not have bloodshot eyes and tear-stained cheeks.

"No," Emma-Jean said. "I do not think you are fine."

Colleen's smile quivered, then collapsed over her braces.

"You're right, Emma-Jean," Colleen whispered. "The truth is I'm not doing well at all. I'm having some trouble, bad trouble, with some of my friends. . . ." Colleen shook her head. "Some people . . . aren't nice."

Emma-Jean knew this was true. People sometimes behaved unkindly toward one another, even at William Gladstone Middle School. Hurt feelings, bruised egos, broken promises, betrayed confidences— the list of emotional injuries her fellow seventh graders inflicted on one another was dismayingly long.

Of course, Emma-Jean was fond of her peers.

In fact, she believed that one was unlikely to find a finer group of young people than the 103 boys and 98 girls with whom she spent her school days. But their behavior was often irrational. And as a result, their lives were messy. Emma-Jean disliked disorder of any kind, and had thus made it her habit to keep herself separate, to observe from afar.

Colleen looked at herself in the mirror and gasped. "Oh my gosh! Look at me! I look like a monster!"

Emma-Jean leaned forward and inspected Colleen's reflection. She saw nothing monstrous. Colleen's eyes were merely red and swollen, which was to be expected of a person in a distressed emotional state. Emma-Jean went to the paper towel dispenser and pulled out a length of the scratchy brown paper. She wet it, folded it into a perfect rectangle, and held it out to Colleen.

"Put this on your eyes," Emma-Jean said. "It will minimize the redness and swelling."

This treatment had always worked well for Emma-Jean's mother, who cried for several hours every July 2 and for several more every November 3.

July 2 was the birthday of Eugene Lazarus, Emma-Jean's father. November 3 was the anniversary of his death. He died two years, three months, and fourteen days ago, when Emma-Jean was ten, in a car accident on I-95. He had been on his way home from a math conference, where he had submitted his award-winning paper on the legendary French mathematician Jules Henri Poincaré.

Colleen accepted the wet towel and held it against her eyes. To promote an atmosphere of calm, Emma-Jean stood very still with her hands folded in front of her pressed khakis. All was silent except for the slow drip of the right-hand sink.

"It's all Laura's fault," Colleen whispered. "Laura Gilroy."

Emma-Jean nodded, for she too often found Laura Gilroy to be disturbing. She was bossy and loud and slammed her locker. Every day at recess, Laura led a group of seventh-grade girls, including Colleen, through a series of dance routines. If someone stumbled or did the wrong move (often it was Colleen who tripped or missed a choreographed kick or turn), Laura would laugh and call them unkind names, such as klutz or spaz. When Laura grew tired of dancing, she would run to the basketball court and snatch the ball from Will Keeler and his friends. Then she would gallop around the blacktop screaming, "Try to get me! Try to get me!"

Emma-Jean wasn't the least bit surprised that Laura Gilroy could cause Colleen Pomerantz to cry.

"The thing is," Colleen said, pressing the paper towels against her eyes, "Laura is trying to steal Kaitlin from me."

Kaitlin was Kaitlin Vogel.

"Kaitlin's my best friend, did you know that?"

Of course Emma-Jean knew. She knew just about everything about her fellow seventh graders.

"And every single February, the last weekend, I go with Kaitlin and her parents up to ski in Vermont. But Laura got it in her head that she should go this year. Instead of me. And Laura can be so . . . powerful that somehow she got Kaitlin to invite her."

Colleen shivered, though the girls' room was stuffy and warm.

"The thing is," she continued, "I'm the one who loves to ski! I'm the one who loves Kaitlin! And I'm the one who Kaitlin really wants to be with!"

"That is obvious," Emma-Jean said.

Colleen removed the paper towel from her eyes and regarded Emma-Jean with keen interest. "You think so?"

"Of course," Emma-Jean said. "She always saves you a chair in the cafeteria, and won't let anyone else sit there, even when you are late."

"That's true," Colleen said. "She did that today."

"Kaitlin has great affection for you," Emma-Jean said. "I am certain."

Colleen threw the used paper towel into the trash receptacle. She took a deep breath and exhaled a cloud of bubble-gum-scented breath that made Emma-Jean blink. "Thanks, Emma-Jean," she said with a tremulous smile. "You're really nice to say all that."

The bell rang, signaling the beginning of last period. Emma-Jean picked up Colleen's backpack, which was bright pink like most of the items in Colleen's wardrobe. Emma-Jean handed the backpack to Colleen and then picked up her own schoolbag, the leather briefcase that had belonged to her father. The leather was worn in places, but it was roomy enough to hold Emma-Jean's meticulous notebooks and sketchbook, her favorite pen and two sharp pencils, and a metal thermos containing her lunch.

Emma-Jean was turning toward the door when Colleen grabbed her by the hand.

"Oh gosh, I can't. I can't go out there. I just can't. Oh . . . Emma-Jean, please help me."

Emma-Jean froze, as startled by the warmth of Colleen's hand as by her unexpected words.

Help me.

Colleen dropped Emma-Jean's hand and rushed back to the sink. She turned her back on Emma-Jean and cried with renewed vigor. Emma-Jean was unsure how to proceed. She maintained a general policy of staying out of the messy lives of her fellow seventh graders. But never before had one of them directly appealed to her for assistance.

Emma-Jean thought of Jules Henri Poincaré, her

father's hero. The legendary French mathematician believed that even the most complex problems could be solved through a process of creative thinking. It was true that Poincaré worked on chaos theory and celestial mechanics, not the interpersonal problems of seventh-grade girls. But what if a kind and cheerful seventh grader like Colleen Pomerantz had asked for his help? Emma-Jean believed Poincaré would have accepted the challenge.

An unusual surge of energy came over Emma-Jean, very possibly a thrill, as she took a step toward Colleen. She had the feeling of walking through an invisible door, the door that had always seemed to separate her from her fellow seventh graders.

Surprisingly, the door was wide open.

Chapter 2

An alarm went off in Colleen Pomerantz's brain, and it was way louder than the Hello Kitty alarm clock that had woken her up at 6:30 that morning, when everything seemed really perfect or pretty good or at least okay.

Oh gosh! Colleen! Get a grip! You are sobbing in the bathroom and everyone is going to find out and they're all going to think that you are crazy!

Colleen held on to the sink. She took some more deep breaths, which were supposed to be relaxing but were not at all relaxing. A minute ago she thought she could pull herself together, that she could go out there and face the world.

But now . . .

Oh gosh, she felt sick.

She could faint!

Or throw up!

In the girls' room!

People would laugh as she walked through the halls. They would stare at her and whisper things while she ate her turkey and nonfat cheese sandwich. They'd make up a horrible name for her, like Crazy Colleen, or Crazy Throw-up Colleen (Colleen was bad at thinking up nicknames, but some people were really good at it).

Then a voice whispered in Colleen's head:

Emma-Jean Lazarus won't tell anyone.

Oh gosh.

It was true.

Emma-Jean Lazarus was probably the only person in the whole school who wouldn't go around blabbing about Colleen's breakdown in the bathroom.

Colleen looked at Emma-Jean. Really looked. Right then Emma-Jean didn't look weird. She looked kind and wise, a little like the statue of the Virgin Mary at Colleen's church.

And why hadn't Colleen ever noticed how pretty Emma-Jean was? Her long brown hair was totally thick and shiny and had way more natural body than Colleen's. Emma-Jean's skin was perfectly smooth. And look at her eyes, how pretty, bright green with little sparkles of blue, like Kaitlin's cat's.

Colleen studied *Teen Beauty* magazine each and every month, and right then she realized Emma-Jean would be totally perfect for their "Beauty Police" section, where the editors kidnap someone off the street and give her a total makeover. Emma-Jean had natural beauty but no style.

Colleen might have even said this to Emma-Jean, right then and there, but Colleen was pretty sure Emma-Jean didn't care about things like makeup. And Colleen had to admit that a makeover probably wouldn't make much difference anyway. There was something a little strange about Emma-Jean, something Colleen couldn't put her finger on but also couldn't really ignore, even if she tried. Like the way

Emma-Jean was staring at her right now. The weird way she talked. She'd always been a little peculiar. For as long as Colleen could remember, kids had snickered about Emma-Jean behind her back.

But never Colleen!

Colleen would never make fun of someone, no matter how weird they acted. Colleen wasn't the prettiest girl in the seventh grade, or the smartest. She wasn't the best artist or the best violin player or the best dresser. But Colleen Pomerantz was nice. Really, really, really, really nice. Maybe even the nicest girl in the seventh grade, though she would never want to brag. Colleen had this idea—a faded, crumpled, smudged idea—that being nice counted for something, even in the seventh grade.

The truth was that Colleen admired Emma-Jean, and not because Emma-Jean was a total genius who got straight A's.

Emma-Jean was amazing to Colleen because Emma-Jean didn't seem to care what people thought of her. This not caring made Emma-Jean seem almost superhuman to Colleen. Truly, if Colleen could be a superhero with just one power, she wouldn't want to fly or see through walls or lift cars with one finger. Colleen would want the power not to care. And her name would be . . . *Super Not-Care Girl*.

Oh, it would be so great to go through one day— one hour!—not worrying that someone was mad at her, or if a joke she told was completely lame. If only she could be more like Emma-Jean. If only Colleen hadn't cried for three days when she wasn't invited to Neil Messner's bar mitzvah. Emma-Jean wasn't invited (Kaitlin got the whole guest list, so Colleen knew this for sure). And yet Colleen was sure that Emma-Jean didn't rush home every day praying she'd find a blue and silver envelope in the mailbox.

As far as Colleen knew, the only party that Emma-Jean had ever been invited to had been Colleen's own fifth-grade Halloween party. Colleen had invited her whole class because unlike some of the girls, Colleen would never not invite someone just because that person was sort of strange and spent recess staring at trees.

Emma-Jean had come dressed as Albert Einstein, with a crazy gray wig and glasses and a T-shirt with some math writing on it, like E + 2 = 5. Emma-Jean's dad had come with her, Colleen remembered. How could she forget? Mr. Lazarus wasn't like the other parents, who'd dropped off their kids and then waved good-bye. He had come right in and joined the party. He had bobbed for apples alongside Emma-Jean. When Colleen had put on the song "Monster Mash," Mr. Lazarus had held Emma-Jean's hands and danced with her. Emma-Jean had laughed so hard, her Einstein wig had fallen off. At first, Mr. Lazarus had seemed a little, well, sort of odd. Like Emma-Jean. But it turned out he was really, really sweet, the way he'd helped Colleen's mom cut the cake so that there were exactly twenty-four pieces, all perfect squares, and how he complimented Colleen on her hula girl costume, even though her mom had made her wear a T-shirt under it and she looked pretty dorky. When it was time to leave, Emma-Jean's dad said good-bye to everyone and remembered every single kid's name.

Oh gosh! Emma-Jean's dad!

Colleen suddenly remembered that just a few days after the party, Mr. Lazarus had . . . He was . . .

Poor Emma-Jean!

Colleen actually felt a stab in her heart, like some mini angel was jabbing it, reminding her how selfish she was acting, obsessing over this stupid situation in front of Emma-Jean, who had lost her father! Colleen had to pull herself together!

"You've already helped me so much, Emma-Jean, just by listening to me," Colleen said. "I'm really lucky you were here."

"Yes," Emma-Jean said. "It was a fortunate coincidence."

Just then, the door of the girls' room opened and a blond frizzy head peeped inside.

Kaitlin!

"Colleen!" Kaitlin said. "I've been looking everywhere for you!"

"Oh . . ." Colleen wasn't sure what to say. Should she tell Kaitlin how hurt she was? That she had almost fainted? Should she be mad at Kaitlin for being kind of a bad friend?

"Coll?" Kaitlin said, pushing her eyebrows together like she did when she was really worried. "Are you okay? Are you sick? What's wrong?"

No, Colleen shouldn't be mad. Kaitlin didn't hurt Colleen on purpose, right? Kaitlin was under Laura's wicked spell.

Colleen put on her sunniest smile.

"I'm fine!" she said. "Let's go!"

Kaitlin held the door open for Colleen.

"See you later, Emma-Jean," Colleen said, waving. "Thanks!"

"You can be confident that your problem will be resolved," Emma-Jean said.

As the door was swishing shut behind them, Kaitlin leaned into Colleen and whispered, "*What* is wrong with Emma-Jean Lazarus?"

Chapter 3

Emma-Jean had excellent hearing and had heard Kaitlin Vogel's whispered question. She'd also heard Colleen's response. "Oh nothing," Colleen had said. "Emma-Jean's just a little . . . she's just different." Which was precisely what Emma-Jean would have said. For it was quite obvious that Emma-Jean was different from most people. She was more rational, less prone to be carried away by emotion or whim. Emma-Jean considered herself lucky to have been born with an exceptionally steady nature, though there were times when the differences between herself and her peers presented some challenges.

When she was much younger, spending time

with other children often left her feeling confused, as though she were visiting with creatures of a different species. In kindergarten, she had spent each recess perched at the top of the monkey bars, watching her buzz-cut and pigtailed peers chasing each other around the playground. It was odd the way they screamed as though they were scared, yet smiled as if they were happy. A group of girls might yell to a boy, "Dylan!" but when Dylan walked over, the girls would run away shrieking and laughing. Emma-Jean would study Dylan, wondering what was frightening about him, or, alternatively, what was funny. Perhaps they suspected he had pinkeye. But then why call him over and risk infection? Or maybe he had been muttering an amusing rhyme that Emma-Jean couldn't hear. Each new situation was like a puzzle that Emma-Jean had to solve.

Emma-Jean had observed her peers closely over the years. Her painstaking research had given her a much clearer understanding of their complex emotional lives and surprising sensitivities. With steady practice, and help from her father and mother,

Emma-Jean had learned how to interact with her schoolmates in a manner that minimized confusion on all sides.

But of course her peers were unpredictable—this was their nature. And even now, every so often, Emma-Jean would have an experience that pushed her to the limits of her understanding.

For example, there had been an incident that took place just a few weeks before, in the cafeteria. Emma-Jean had been eating her soup, alone as usual, when a boy named Brandon Mahoney approached her. He was holding a pear, which he held out for Emma-Jean. He was grinning so widely that Emma-Jean could see his many fillings. It was not surprising that Brandon Mahoney did not practice good dental hygiene, since his locker was filled with trash and his fingernails were dirty and ragged.

He looked back over his shoulder and said, "This is for you. It's from Will Keeler."

Emma-Jean appreciated the pear, which was large and unblemished and would, following a rigorous washing, make a tasty snack for her walk home.

It did strike her as unusual that Will Keeler would want to give the pear to her, since he had never spoken to her, even when they sat across from each other in art class last quarter. Then again, perhaps he, like she, had observed what other students customarily ate for lunch, and thus knew that Emma-Jean always had at least one piece of fruit.

"You may tell Will that I appreciate the pear," Emma-Jean said.

For some reason Brandon Mahoney seemed to find this statement amusing, since he began to laugh. Emma-Jean couldn't imagine what was funny, and before she could ask Brandon, Will Keeler appeared. Brandon and Will were friends. But now Will didn't look the least bit amiable. In fact, he was looking at Brandon with a most disapproving expression, his large blue eyes narrowed, his lips pressed tight together. Emma-Jean wondered if Will regretted that Brandon had given away his pear.

Emma-Jean picked up the pear and handed it to Will. "You may have this back, if you're still hungry."

Brandon was now laughing so hard that his entire face had turned the color of Emma-Jean's tomato soup. "She . . . is . . . so . . . strange!" he gasped.

Will took a step toward Brandon. Will was taller than most of the seventh-grade boys, and he towered over Brandon. "You're an idiot," he said. He was gripping the pear so tightly that his knuckles were white. Emma-Jean feared the pear would become bruised.

"Whoa!" Brandon said, breaking into a sprint away from Will and Emma-Jean.

Will hesitated for just a moment before hurling the pear at Brandon. It shot through the air, a green blur. Brandon inopportunely turned and looked at Will at exactly the second of impact. The pear struck him, with tremendous force, squarely in the forehead. Brandon fell, crashing into several metal chairs on his way to the floor. Emma-Jean was so startled by the noise that she nearly knocked over her thermos. Seconds later, Mr. Petrowski appeared, pointing at Will and shouting, "I saw that! I saw the whole thing!" He escorted Will to the office, and

Will was sent home for the remainder of the day.

Emma-Jean puzzled over this incident for much of the afternoon. She would have still been wondering about it, had it not been for the astute advice of her mother.

Elizabeth Lazarus was younger than the parents of most of Emma-Jean's classmates. Yet she possessed the wisdom of an old sage. She always had keen insights into matters of the human mind and spirit. Over the years, Emma-Jean had engaged her in frequent discussions about her peers. Almost all of these discussions took place in Emma-Jean's mother's bed, to which Emma-Jean and her mother often retreated in the later hours of the evening to read and discuss the day's events.

That evening, as was her habit, Emma-Jean had brought into bed the quilt her father had made for her when she was born. It was made of hundreds of tiny squares, arranged in a pattern of startling intricacy. She and her mother liked to warm their feet under the soft cotton, mindful not to get their toes caught in the ragged edges. Emma-Jean knew that she needed to repair the quilt's border, that it could fall apart if she didn't. Her mother had brought her many times to the crafts store, but Emma-Jean had yet to find an assortment of fabrics that would fit with her father's pattern.

Emma-Jean recounted the cafeteria incident, sparing no detail. Her mother listened closely, her coppery eyes intense. When Emma-Jean finished talking, her mother took a few moments to reflect, pursing her lips in concentration. Emma-Jean waited patiently, at one point reaching over to gently remove a piece of lint from one of her mother's reddish curls.

"I feel sorry for Brandon," her mother announced.

"Why?" Emma-Jean said.

"Because I can picture him as an adult," her mother said.

Emma-Jean's mother would never claim to possess anything as fanciful as psychic powers. But she did have the ability to project into the future with surprising accuracy. For instance, as she had told Emma-Jean many times, she had known instantly that Eugene Lazarus should be her husband. They met when Emma-Jean's father was opening a checking account at the bank where Emma-Jean's mother worked. This was before Emma-Jean's mother began her steady climb through the bank hierarchy, and just weeks after her father had graduated from M.I.T. and moved to town to begin his doctoral work at the university.

"Your father was very shy back then," her mother had told her. "But I could see what was inside him. It was all written out in those eyes of his, that he was a man who had a gift for life. Like you have, Emma-Jean. It was all right there, waiting for a person who would know how to open that gift. And that person was me."

Of course her mother had been right.

Emma-Jean tried now to imagine Brandon Mahoney grown up. She frowned as she pictured a man with several missing teeth and bleeding gums, whose ill-advised antics provoked generally good-natured people into acts of violence involving fruit.

Her mother was correct. Life could not turn out well for such a person.

"What about Will Keeler?" Emma-Jean said.

"I like him," her mother said without hesitation.

"But you've never met him," Emma-Jean said.

"I still like him," her mother said. "I believe he was defending your honor."

"Like a knight?" Emma-Jean said, incredulous.

"Yes," Emma-Jean's mother said. "Just like a knight."

Emma-Jean was speechless. Her father had read her many volumes of Arthurian legends. She had never considered that a boy like Will Keeler could have anything in common with the chivalrous warriors of medieval times.

Then again, Emma-Jean recalled that many of the bravest knights were simple men who ate mutton with their fingers and bathed but once a year. Perhaps there was more to Will Keeler than mediocre grades and exceptional basketball skills. Perhaps he possessed a talent for old-fashioned gallantry that went largely unnoticed in the modern hallways of William Gladstone Middle School.

Emma-Jean would have to observe him more closely.

"What about what Brandon said," Emma-Jean said, "that I am strange."

Emma-Jean's mother sat up.

"Let's look up the word *strange* in the dictionary and see if he is correct," she suggested, brushing a hair from Emma-Jean's forehead.

They both rose from the bed and went over to their well-worn copy of the *Oxford English Dictionary,* kept out on her mother's dresser for handy reference.

There was a large entry for the word *strange*, but Emma-Jean's mother pointed to the second definition:

> **strange** *adj*
> extraordinary, remarkable, singular

"Do you think this is an accurate description of you?" her mother said.

Emma-Jean let the words seep in and settle in her mind. They fit quite well.

"Very accurate."

"I agree," her mother said, closing the dictionary and patting the sky blue cover. "The next time someone calls you strange, you should thank them. It sounds to me like a compliment."

Emma-Jean nodded.

"Did people think my father was strange?" Emma-Jean asked, sitting back down on the bed and wrapping the quilt around her shoulders. It gave her a feeling of deep comfort.

"Oh yes," her mother said, smiling slightly and looking at the large photograph of Eugene Lazarus that sat in a brass frame by the bedside. Though her father had died over two years ago, he still watched over them. There were pictures of him in every room of the house. They were framed on the walls, stuck to mirrors, hung with magnets on the refrigerator, slipped into the pages of novels. Her mother kept a small snapshot tucked into the sun visor of her Toyota Corolla.

"Your father was wonderfully strange," her mother

said. "He was an absolute original. Like you. That's one of the reasons I loved him so much, and one of the many, many, many reasons why I love you."

Emma-Jean was always pleased to hear that she took after her father, a brilliant mathematician, a beloved professor, and the love of her mother's life.

Emma-Jean had looked at her father's photograph, focusing on his bright green eyes, which peered merrily out from under a mop of shaggy black hair. As always, he seemed to give her a reassuring nod.

Chapter 4

Emma-Jean began working on Colleen Pomerantz's problem without delay. During lunch that day, she outlined Colleen's problem from all angles. By the time the bell rang, she had conceived of a multistepped, highly logical plan of action.

Step one required her to stay after school in order to study the large bulletin board outside the main office. This was where flyers were posted announcing important news and upcoming events. Emma-Jean looked carefully at all the notices until she found the one she was looking for.

BOYS' BASKETBALL AWARDS BANQUET

THE BANQUET FOR THE BOYS' PAL BASKETBALL TEAM WILL BE HELD THIS SATURDAY NIGHT, FEBRUARY 24, IN THE SCHOOL GYM, FROM 6:00—8:30

Emma-Jean copied the information into her notebook and hurried home to Stanton Drive. Her house was a small Victorian that she and her mother had recently repainted robin's egg blue with pale yellow trim. The house had many good qualities, in particular the dogwood tree she and her father had planted outside her bedroom window the spring before he died. Emma-Jean and her father had spent long afternoons drawing the tree, making note of new branches and shoots.

Another fine quality was the delicious smell of garlic and curry spices that greeted Emma-Jean when she came home from school each day. The person responsible for this aroma was Vikram Adwani, who was the best cook Emma-Jean had ever known. He was thirty-one years old and six feet tall and came from Mumbai, India. He had caramel-colored skin and a long black ponytail. He was a doctoral student in immunology at the university, and for close to six months, he had rented the sunny third floor of Emma-Jean's house.

Emma-Jean hung up her coat and stopped into the kitchen to visit Vikram, who was standing at the stove, stirring the contents of a cast-iron skillet. He smiled at Emma-Jean.

"I'm sorry I can't assist you today," Emma-Jean said. "I am helping one of my classmates solve a serious problem."

"Very good," Vikram said, holding out a wooden spoon full of chana masala for Emma-Jean to sample. Emma-Jean admired the attractive combination of the golden chickpeas and crimson tomatoes. She blew on the spoon a few times to clear the rising steam, and took a taste. She closed her eyes as her senses filled with a lively blend of flavors—turmeric, she thought, and certainly cumin, and just the right amount of chili pepper. Emma-

Jean nodded her approval and put the spoon in the sink.

"Your flavors are perfectly balanced," she said.

"That's kind of you to say," Vikram said

"I will be in my room."

"Good luck with your problem," Vikram said, lowering the gas flame under his pan.

"It is a challenging one."

"I have great confidence in you."

"Thank you," Emma-Jean said.

Emma-Jean went upstairs to her neat and airy bedroom, where she was greeted by the soft squawking of Henri, a seventeen-year-old parakeet. Henri had been her father's bird, named, of course, for Poincaré.

"Emma-Jean," the bird said in his raspy whisper. "Greetings, Emma-Jean. *Bonjour. Hola. Namaste.*"

Emma-Jean unlatched the door of the cage and stood still as the bird flew out and settled on her shoulder. Henri leaned his soft, tidy head against her cheek. Emma-Jean closed her eyes. Her days were filled with pleasant moments, and this was one she particularly relished.

"I'm sorry, dear Henri, but I can't talk right now," Emma-Jean said in a low voice. "We'll have time to talk later. Right now, I have an important and challenging problem to tend to."

With Henri on her shoulder, Emma-Jean sat at her computer and gathered her thoughts. Using the computer program Quark Xpress, Emma-Jean painstakingly re-created the William Gladstone Middle School logo, which included the school's name written in eighteen-point Times New Roman font, framed by a royal blue rectangular box.

She printed out a sheet of paper with the school's logo on top. Then she composed a letter. It took her several drafts to achieve the correct wording and tone, but as the afternoon was fading to evening, she printed out her final version.

Ms. Laura Gilroy
3 Feather Place
River Flats, CT 07890

Dear Laura,

It is my pleasure to inform you that you have been selected to perform at the boys' basketball awards banquet on Saturday night, February 24. There will be a short dance performance following the awards presentation, and several talented dancers from various grades have been invited to perform. You are the only seventh-grade dancer selected, and we ask that you keep this matter quiet until after the banquet.

You must attend a rehearsal on Friday night, at 8 p.m. in the school gym. We apologize for the last-minute notice, and hope you will be able to perform at the banquet. If you can't, we will select an alternate.

Sincerely,
Basketball Banquet Committee

Emma-Jean was a studious observer of human behavior. She had seen enough to deduce that Laura Gilroy would gladly give up the ski trip with Kaitlin Vogel for the opportunity to dance on a stage in front of the boys' basketball team. Laura Gilroy was like a peacock that lived for the chance to display her feathers. Of course Emma-Jean knew it was the male peacock that had the beautiful feathers. But still, she felt the comparison was valid.

Emma-Jean sat back in her chair. She had approached this problem with creativity and logic. However, there were many variables and it was difficult to predict what the outcome would be. Emma-Jean turned to Henri for reassurance, but he was peacefully asleep on her shoulder.

Chapter 5

Colleen's mom had a saying: Time heals all wounds. That's what she'd said when Colleen's hamster died in second grade, and when Colleen didn't make the travel soccer team in fifth grade. And so Colleen knew what to expect when she told her mother that she wasn't going skiing with Kaitlin this year, that Kaitlin was bringing someone else. Colleen half hoped her mother would come over and put her arms around her and pat her back and say, "That's just the worst story I've heard all day! You must feel so hurt!"

But her mother wasn't the huggy type. Besides, she had been busy emptying the dishwasher.

"There will be other ski trips," she'd said, handing Colleen a stack of plates to put in the cabinet. "I know you're upset, but remember . . ." Colleen had cringed, knowing what was coming. "Time heals all wounds."

Okay.

But how much time? Her mother never said. The truth was Colleen still missed Piggy, her adorable hamster who used to tickle her neck with his whiskers. And it was still pretty embarrassing that Colleen was practically the only girl in the entire fifth grade who didn't make the travel team. (Okay, she hated soccer, but all her friends were doing it, and would it have been so hard for the coaches to add just one more girl?)

When would Colleen ever get over this ski trip?

Colleen wondered this as she sat in first-period Spanish, four desks away from Laura Gilroy. It had been two days since Kaitlin had broken the terrible news (two days, 48 hours, 2,880 minutes, 172,800 seconds—Colleen had secretly used her calculator while Señora Weingart was writing on the board).

And Colleen still felt completely, totally miserable.

Spanish was a cinch, and usually Colleen spent the period passing little notes written in pink Magic Marker. Nothing earth-shattering, just sunny little messages to brighten someone's day. *"I luv your sox!"* she might write to her friend Valerie, who could get down on herself. *"Where'd U get them?"*

But Colleen's pink Magic Marker stayed in her backpack. Once she reached for it. Her friend Michele had gotten braces, and Colleen wanted to assure her that she looked as gorgeous as ever. But then the thought of Laura Gilroy skiing down Stratton Mountain played through her mind like a late-night horror movie, and the bright and sunny words in her mind turned to black puffs of smoke.

Colleen looked down at her Spanish notebook, which was covered with doodled hearts and flowers and her name, Colleen Julianna Pomerantz, in her neatest bubble writing. Tears came to her eyes. Why did she have to take everything so hard? Why did she care so much about this ski trip? Why couldn't she be like everyone else and NOT CARE so much? About everything!

"*¿Señorita Pomerantz, te gusta el pastel de chocolate?*"

Oh gosh! What was Señora Wiengart saying!

"Um, sorry, *lo siento mucho, Señora* . . ." Colleen said, trying to perk herself up.

"Señorita Pomerantz," her teacher said, shaking her finger. "*¡Atención!*"

Michele looked over, flashing her braces in sympathy, which was really sweet. Colleen shrugged and gave a little smile back to show that it didn't really bother her that she'd been totally humiliated.

Colleen took a deep breath, filling her nostrils with the Wild at Heart cologne she'd put on this morning. Who was she kidding? Her heart was about as wild as a Twinkie.

Colleen slumped in her seat. Sometimes all her caring and wondering really did make her sick to her stomach. She was pathetic! Why couldn't she stop?

Or why couldn't some people just act nicer?

The bell rang and Colleen gathered up her books, bracing herself for her walk through the hallway, when no matter how bad she felt, she had to put on a smile and say a friendly hello to everyone who walked by.

But then an unbelievable thing happened.

Laura was waiting for Colleen at the door. "Hey," Laura whispered, putting her face so close that Colleen could feel the heat coming off Laura's bronzed skin. "Do you think Kaitlin will hate me if I don't go skiing?"

Just like that.

Colleen leaned against the doorway because fainting was a definite possibility.

Laura reached into her sweatshirt pocket and pulled out one of the fancy little chocolate bars she carried around. Laura made a big deal telling everyone how her father brought them back from his business trips to Switzerland and that they were way better than anything you could get here. Sometimes she shared them, but not too often, and hardly ever with Colleen. Last week, on Valentine's Day, Laura had snuck a whole box into Will Keeler's backpack when he wasn't looking.

Laura held out the chocolate to Colleen. "Something came up and I can't go," she said. "So do you think she'll, like, totally hate me for life?"

For days, Colleen had been surrounded by a cloud of confusion and misery that made everything look foggy.

Now the fog lifted, and Colleen could see it all perfectly. She saw that Laura Gilroy didn't give one hoot about skiing. Or about Kaitlin. And of course she didn't care about Colleen. All Laura Gilroy cared about was Laura Gilroy.

Colleen stared at Laura. She waved away the chocolate because nothing of Laura's could ever taste sweet.

"What?" Laura said.

There were so many answers to that simple question, so many things Colleen wanted to say to Laura at that moment. And one of them was "Thank you." Because right then, at that thrilling moment, Colleen felt free. Everything was so crystal clear! Laura

Gilroy was prettier than Colleen. She was a better dancer. But Colleen had the better heart. And wasn't that the most important thing?

But because she was, above all, a very nice person, Colleen didn't tell Laura Gilroy what she was thinking, and she swallowed the mean words that were lined up on the tip of her tongue. She wanted to walk away, march off without so much as a wave. She'd love to do that!

But she couldn't. "Nothing," Colleen said in not such a nice voice. "I'm sure Kaitlin will be okay."

By the end of the day, Kaitlin had invited Colleen to go skiing. The two had hugged and jumped up and down with excitement.

"I'm so glad she cancelled," Kaitlin whispered. "I was praying she would!"

"You were?" Colleen said.

"I'm so sorry!" Kaitlin said. "Can you forgive me?"

"What a question!" Colleen said.

It was late that night, as Colleen was about to fall asleep, that she remembered her talk with Emma-

Jean Lazarus in the bathroom. A completely weird idea came into Colleen's mind: Had Emma-Jean done something to make Laura change her mind?

Colleen flipped over onto her back and stared at the hearts and stars mobile above her bed.

But how could Emma-Jean have gotten Laura Gilroy to cancel the trip? Emma-Jean was in her own world and had probably forgotten all about Colleen's problems. Colleen closed her eyes. No, she told herself, drifting toward a happy sleep, Laura probably just found something better to do for the weekend.

Chapter 6

There were strong indications that Emma-Jean's plan to solve Colleen's problem had succeeded. The first came on Wednesday before dismissal, when Emma-Jean saw Colleen and Kaitlin standing at Colleen's locker. They had their hands on each other's shoulders and were hopping up and down. It was clear they were celebrating something, since they'd done the same dance when they were voted co–vice secretaries of the seventh-grade class.

Could Colleen and Kaitlin be celebrating Laura Gilroy's decision to abandon the ski trip? Emma-Jean thought this was highly likely, yet she lacked conclusive evidence. On Friday afternoon, Emma-

Jean noted that Colleen Pomerantz did not board her regular bus. She waited in the pickup lane with Kaitlin Vogel. Several minutes later, the Vogel station wagon drove up, with skis attached to the roof. Kaitlin and Colleen both entered the car, and Emma-Jean presumed that they were heading straight for Vermont.

Still, Emma-Jean couldn't be certain of the cause/effect relationship between the letter she had sent to Laura Gilroy and Colleen Pomerantz's presence on the Vogel ski trip.

That evening, after helping her mother and Vikram with the dinner dishes, Emma-Jean announced that she wished to take a short after-dinner walk. The streets of the neighborhood were quiet and safe. She and her father had often ventured into the darkness, hand in hand, to observe their favorite trees in the moonlight, to listen for owls and skunks and other nocturnal creatures, to marvel at the starlit sky that had so inspired Jules Henri Poincaré.

Her mother reminded Emma-Jean to stay on the sidewalks and Emma-Jean zipped up her parka and set out into the cold night.

It took just ten minutes to walk to William Gladstone Middle School. There was only one car in the parking lot, and not a person in sight. She concealed herself behind a boxwood hedge in front of the school, kneeling on a pile of wood chips.

Five minutes later, a tan Ford Expedition sped through the parking lot and pulled up by the front door, a few yards from where Emma-Jean was hiding. The passenger door opened and Laura Gilroy hopped out, slammed the door, and ran into the school.

Emma-Jean waited behind the hedge, leaning against the wall. She could feel the cold bricks through her parka. Just a few minutes later, Laura Gilroy reappeared. She fished a cell phone from her purse and jabbed at the buttons. "There's been a total screwup," she shouted into the phone. "And I need you to pick me up." She stamped a foot. "No! Not fifteen minutes. I look like an idiot! Pick me up RIGHT NOW!"

Laura stuffed the phone back into her purse and paced back and forth across the sidewalk, muttering profanities. She pulled violently on the rear end of her spandex pants, which looked very tight and uncomfortable indeed.

Several minutes later, the tan Expedition reappeared, screeching to a stop where Laura stood, arms crossed, foot tapping. Laura wrenched open the car door, hurled her body up into the front seat, and slammed the door shut.

After the car had sped away, Emma-Jean emerged from her hiding place. She brushed off the wood chips and pine needles that clung to her parka and adjusted the creases of her khakis. She stood very still as she tried to slow the flow of thoughts that rushed through her mind. Her heart was beating rapidly, and despite the cold, she was sweating.

The sight of Laura Gilroy in distress had made Emma-Jean uneasy. Never before, as far as she knew, had Emma-Jean ever purposefully done something that had caused another person to be angry or upset.

Emma-Jean stared into the darkness, processing her thoughts.

It was not desirable to cause someone distress,

even someone as thoughtless—perhaps even malevolent—as Laura Gilroy. But the facts were clear enough: Laura had created a problem. And Emma-Jean had solved it. Right now, Colleen was somewhere in the mountains of Vermont, enjoying her rightful place alongside her best friend. And though Laura had been upset, her pitiless spirit would rebound quickly.

Slowly, the confusion in her mind dissipated like an early-morning mist. Emma-Jean's heart rate slowed. Rational thought had returned.

In a small way, Emma-Jean believed her actions had helped restore balance to the chaotic universe of the William Gladstone seventh grade.

Emma-Jean reflected on these remarkable events as she walked along the quiet streets of her neighborhood and under the arching elms. When she got home, she made herself a cup of tea and ate an apple. According to her father's book, this was how Jules Henri Poincaré marked the successful completion of a challenging mathematical problem.

Chapter 7

Emma-Jean was so pleased with the positive resolution of Colleen's problem that she decided to lend her assistance to others should the opportunity arise. Fortuitously, another problem came to her attention the very next week.

She was in the cafeteria. As usual, Emma-Jean was sitting at a large round table by herself, surrounded by the not unpleasant clamor and buzz of her fellow seventh graders. She had just opened her thermos and was enjoying the first spoonful of her tomato soup when the sound of Mr. Petrowski's blustery voice broke her mood of calm. He was standing just a few feet away from Emma-Jean, speaking to

Ms. Wright, Emma-Jean's language arts teacher. They hadn't noticed Emma-Jean, since they were separated from her by a vending machine.

"What I'm saying is that Will Keeler stole my candy," said the science teacher. "He went into the teachers' lounge and took it right from my locker. I don't know how he did it, but believe you me it was him, and I'm going to nail him."

"That sounds odd," said Ms. Wright. "How do you know it was he?"

"I caught him eating chocolate in class. Right in front of me."

"That doesn't mean he stole your chocolate, Phil," Ms. Wright said. "Really, Will Keeler doesn't strike me as the criminal type."

"You kidding me?" Mr. Petrowski said. "He's bad news, that kid. You know what he did to Brandon Mahoney, don't you? Brandon could have ended up in the emergency room."

"Really, Phil," Ms. Wright said. "Brandon Mahoney could make anyone throw a pear at him. And Will Keeler is a good kid."

"Well, I think you're naïve."

Ms. Wright was much younger than Mr. Petrowski, and she was new this year to William Gladstone Middle School. Still, Emma-Jean knew that she was not naïve. She was intelligent and well traveled; in fact, she had recently visited her mother's relatives in the African country of Ghana. Most strikingly, Ms. Wright was the only teacher who'd ever asked Emma-Jean if she had been named after Emma Lazarus, the woman who wrote the poem inscribed on the Statue of Liberty. Emma-Jean had told her that indeed she had been, that her mother and father decided to get married while visiting the Statue of Liberty.

"They also decided that should they have a daughter, they would always remember the day by naming her Emma."

"And where did the name Jean come from?" Ms. Wright had inquired.

"My father's name is Eugene," Emma-Jean explained. "My mother put Jean on the birth certificate to surprise him."

"It's a wonderful name," Ms. Wright said. "Full of character."

"My parents had only known each other for two weeks when my father proposed to my mother," Emma-Jean told her. "They got married a month later."

"That's so romantic!"

"They were very happy," Emma-Jean said, thinking of the many stories her parents had told her.

The next day, Ms. Wright had asked her to stay behind after the bell rang.

"Emma-Jean," she said in a quiet voice. "Yesterday, when we spoke about your parents, I didn't know that your father had passed away. I wanted to tell you how sorry I am."

"He was very brilliant," Emma-Jean said. "He wrote a book on Jules Henri Poincaré that won the David H. Dreyfuss Prize for Mathematics Scholarship. He taught me all I know about trees."

"I understand he was one of the most popular professors at the university."

"Yes. And he was the love of my mother's life."

"Yes. It must be hard for you to . . ."

"Thank you," Emma-Jean had said as she walked away.

Ms. Wright had not mentioned this topic again, though at Christmastime she had sent Emma-Jean a holiday card in the mail. The card was illustrated with a graceful watercolor of twin cherry trees, their lush blossoms glowing pink, like a sunset reflected on water. Emma-Jean had pasted it into her sketchbook, and still enjoyed looking at it before she went to sleep at night.

Sometimes when Ms. Wright had lunch duty, she would join Emma-Jean at her table for a few minutes, and they could share insights into the book or poem they were reading in class. Emma-Jean hoped Ms. Wright would join her today, and peered around the vending machine to try to catch her eye. However, Mr. Petrowski had shifted his weight, and his hulking body now blocked the willowy Ms. Wright from view.

Emma-Jean watched as Mr. Petrowski leaned closer to Ms. Wright. "Here's what happened," he said. "I went into the lounge and sat on the couch. I dropped my pen and it went between the cushions.

I reached in to get it, and instead I pulled out something slimy and brown."

Emma-Jean made a face.

"A fun-size Milky Way, slightly melted," Mr. Petrowski clarified.

"So?"

"So I got suspicious. I keep a bag of candy in my locker . . . sweet tooth, you know? I got up to check in my locker, and sure enough, there was a hole in my bag and half the candy was gone."

"And you think Will Keeler went into the lounge, broke into your locker, and stole some candy?"

"I do."

"And you think he ate some and put the rest in the couch cushions? That makes absolutely no sense, Phil."

"He probably sat down to have a little snack and dropped a few. A kid like that would have no compunction."

Ms. Wright and Mr. Petrowski both turned and looked into the unruly crowd of boys. Emma-Jean followed their gaze. The boys appeared to be engaged in a lively display of belching.

Belching was considered impolite, Emma-Jean knew, unless one happened to be in China, where a belch was a signal that one was satisfied with his meal. It was possible one of the boys had vacationed in China during February break and was sharing the country's cultural customs with his peers. However, Emma-Jean was skeptical that the William Gladstone Middle School hot lunch could inspire a satisfied sound of any kind.

"Just look at him," Mr. Petrowski said, sneering at Will Keeler.

Emma-Jean looked closely at Will, who was now standing up. He wore his yellow-blond hair shaggy around his ears. His basketball jersey was stained with what appeared to be chocolate milk. Emma-Jean studied Will, hoping to see hints of the Arthurian heart her mother was so certain he possessed. At exactly that moment, Will put his arms out like an opera singer reaching for a high note, and emitted a belch so loud that it rose above the shouts and giggles like a foghorn in a hurricane.

"Phil, excuse me for saying so, but this all sounds

a little crazy to me," Ms. Wright said. "I know Will isn't exactly an academic star, but I really doubt—"

"A kid like that," Mr. Petrowski said, shaking his head. "He has everything handed to him."

"What does that—"

"Haven't you seen the billboards up and down Post Road? Keeler Cadillac? That's the old man. The family's the biggest Caddy dealer on the East Coast. And you know I bought myself a pre-owned Escalade last year. The thing's a lemon. First it was the transmission that went bad, then the air-conditioning, and now there's this rattling noise. Driving me insane!"

"Phil, are you feeling all right?"

Mr. Petrowski did not seem to be listening to Ms. Wright. His eyes were glued to Will Keeler, and he was speaking very fast. "I've had the car serviced five times in three months. I've spent a thousand bucks. Do they care? Not a wink. An average Joe like me? Why would they care? That family's made of money."

"Phil," she said. "Look at me. I can practically assure you that Will Keeler had nothing to do with your missing candy. It's obvious that you are riled up about your car, and . . . really. You need to calm down."

Mr. Petrowski shook his head and waved his hand at Ms. Wright. "You'll see," he said. "After a while you'll get it. You'll see things the way I do."

"I really hope I don't!" Ms. Wright said, turning and walking out of the cafeteria.

Emma-Jean found this conversation disturbing. Whether or not Will Keeler had the makings of a knight, it was clear to her that he was an unlikely thief. In fact, she very much doubted that any of her fellow seventh graders would commit such a crime. Emma-Jean had a hunch, and she decided she needed to stay after school to investigate.

She waited until after the last bus had rumbled out of the parking lot and the hallways were quiet before knocking on the door of the teachers' lounge. When nobody replied, she opened the door, closing it carefully behind her. The lounge was small, with a sink against the back wall, a worn black leather couch on the right, and a row of lockers running the entire length of the left-hand wall. Unlike the metal student lockers that lined the carpeted hallways of William Gladstone, the teachers' lockers were made of wood and were joined together as one long cabinet.

Emma-Jean went to the couch first. She lifted up one of the cushions and wrinkled her lip in distaste at what she saw: crumbs from many varieties of chips, cookies, and crackers. She lifted the other cushions. As she had predicted, there was a mini Snickers bar, still in its wrapper. Mindful of germs, Emma-Jean took a tissue from her pocket and used it to pick up the bar. She inspected it. The wrapper was gnawed at the corner. Emma-Jean wrapped it in the tissue and placed it in the pocket of her cardigan sweater.

Emma-Jean found the locker with a rectangular metal tab engraved *P. Petrowski*. She then walked to the back of the room and tugged on the row of cabinets with both hands. It slid easily away from the wall. She walked slowly behind the cabinets, her eyes scanning the floor. And there it was, the proof she had been seeking. The floor was covered with hundreds of tiny brown beads, which Emma-Jean unmistakably identified as mouse droppings. The wood that backed Mr. Petrowski's cabinet was marred by a hole, chewed around the edges. Emma-Jean judged that the size of the hole would enable a mouse to enter quite easily, and then exit carrying a fun-size Milky Way in his whiskered mouth.

Emma-Jean came out from behind the cabinets. Just then, the door to the teachers' lounge swung open. Emma-Jean froze, knowing that despite her honorable intentions, she was currently trespassing in the teachers' lounge, a serious breech of school rules.

It was thus a relief when the doorway filled with the large figure of Mr. Johannsen, the school custodian. He was, in Emma-Jean's mind, one of the most important members of the William Gladstone Middle School staff. Emma-Jean disliked messes, and appreciated the care with which Mr. Johannsen mopped the cafeteria floor and swept the sidewalks in front of the school.

Emma-Jean tried to make his job easier by picking up the candy wrappers and empty chip bags she often found in the school parking lot. She picked up lunch trays her fellow seventh graders left behind in the cafeteria and pushed in their chairs.

"Well hello there, missy," said Mr. Johannsen. "Can I help you?"

"I'm aware that I am in violation of school rules, Mr. Johannsen," Emma-Jean said. "However, I am currently working to solve the problem of Mr. Petrowski's missing candy."

"You are, are you?"

"Yes. Are you aware of this situation?"

"I am," said Mr. Johannsen, smoothing down what was left of his fluffy white hair. "Crime of the century, you'd think, the way Petrowski's carrying on. You'd think there were diamonds inside those candy bars."

"Diamonds are not edible, Mr. Johannsen. You must know that."

Mr. Johannsen chuckled. "You got me there, Emma-Jean."

"In any event, the candy was not taken by a student," Emma-Jean informed him. "It was taken by a mouse."

"A mouse?" he said, stepping forward.

"Yes. We once had mice in our home, and I'm familiar with their behavior. When I heard about Mr. Petrowski's candy, I suspected it was a mouse."

"You did, did you?" said Mr. Johannsen.

"I found their droppings behind the lockers. I was going to sweep them up."

"You know how I appreciate all of your help."

Mr. Johannsen had once informed her that in all his thirty-four years working as a custodian, he'd never encountered a student as mindful of cleanliness as Emma-Jean.

Emma-Jean motioned for Mr. Johannsen to inspect behind the lockers.

"There's a hole in Mr. Petrowski's locker."

"A hole?"

"May I borrow your flashlight?" she said, pointing to the one that hung from his belt, partially hidden by his large stomach. Mr. Johannsen unclipped his flashlight, turned it on, and handed it to Emma-Jean.

Emma-Jean illuminated the area behind Mr. Petrowski's locker.

"Well, look at that," Mr. Johannsen said.

"And you should also see this," Emma-Jean said, taking the candy bar from her cardigan pocket. "See how this is gnawed?" she said, holding it out to Mr. Johannsen. "I found it in the couch. Mice often move food from one location to another."

"They do, do they?" said Mr. Johannsen.

"Yes," Emma-Jean said. "In my experience they do."

"Well, my dear, you've got a grade-A brain inside that head of yours."

"Thank you, Mr. Johannsen," Emma-Jean said, turning off the flashlight and handing it back to him.

"And a good heart there too," he said.

"Thank you, Mr. Johannsen," Emma-Jean said. "Will you please tell Mr. Petrowski that no student has been stealing his candy?"

"Will do."

"Will you tell him in particular that Will Keeler has not been stealing his candy?"

"I certainly will," Mr. Johannsen said, clipping his flashlight back onto his belt. "And you'd better be heading home."

"Yes," Emma-Jean agreed. "Good-bye, Mr. Johannsen."

"Good-bye, Emma-Jean," he said. "Hey, kids aren't causing you any trouble, now, are they?"

"Of course not," Emma-Jean replied, as usual. She didn't understand why Mr. Johannsen often asked her this odd question. In what way might her fellow seventh graders be any trouble to her? They did not pester her to borrow money for lunch or for answers to the math homework. Occasionally they were loud and rambunctious, and some of the girls did not wash their hands after using the bathroom. But none of this was terribly troubling to Emma-Jean.

"Good. You'll let me know if anyone's causing you trouble, because then they'll have to contend with the likes of me."

Emma-Jean certainly admired Mr. Johannsen, though at times he said perplexing things.

Chapter 8

The following Monday was bright and sunny and many seventh graders rushed through their sandwiches and fish sticks so they could have extra time outside. Emma-Jean took only a few sips of her soup before packing up and seeking her favorite outdoor spot: a bench on the edge of the soccer field. This location placed her out of the range of errant basketballs and beneath the branches of her favorite oak tree. Emma-Jean admired the oak, which had thick twisting branches that reached up into the blue sky. Despite her grounding in modern scientific principles, it was not hard for Emma-Jean to understand how ancient peoples would regard such a creation as a benevolent beast, a guardian of souls.

Emma-Jean saw Colleen Pomerantz on the blacktop. She was with Kaitlin Vogel and her other close friends: an intelligent and high-spirited brunette named Valerie Rosen, and Michele Peters, a tall girl who wore small round glasses and had a fine singing voice. These four girls spent much of their free time in one another's company, and together made up the informal dance troupe led by Laura Gilroy. Emma-Jean was gratified to see that Colleen was smiling, and that her freckled skin had a healthy glow, no doubt a result of her weekend in the mountains.

"Hey, Emma-Jean!" Colleen shouted, waving in her usual animated fashion. "Your hair looks so gorgeous today!"

Emma-Jean nodded in agreement. Due to her well-balanced diet, her hair was thick and glossy and resembled the coat of a Labrador retriever.

The four girls made halfhearted attempts to run through the dance routine they'd been practicing, collapsing into screeching giggles when one of them missed a step. Emma-Jean could not recall any such laughter when Laura was leading them. Usually Laura Gilroy forced them to warm up before dancing, ordering them to twist and stretch their bodies into positions that caused them to grimace and moan.

"Where's Laura?" Valerie asked, echoing Emma-Jean's own thoughts. "She'll kill us for starting without her."

"She wasn't at lunch," Michele said.

"I think I saw her mom at the office," Kaitlin said.

Moments later, Laura appeared, storming across the asphalt.

"I told you guys to wait for me!" she shouted. "You're not supposed to start until I get here!"

"Where were you?" Kaitlin said.

Laura took her usual drill-sergeant stance, feet planted on the ground, hands on her hips.

"You are NOT going to believe this," she announced. "Somebody in this school must think I am a complete moron. They have no IDEA who they are dealing with! You know how I cancelled the ski trip? Well the reason was that I got this letter . . ."

She reached into her back pocket and produced a piece of paper, which she unfolded and held out in front of her. The girls leaned in for a better look. Even from a distance Emma-Jean recognized that it was the letter she had created on falsified William Gladstone Middle School stationery.

"That's so cool!" Colleen said. "No wonder you couldn't go skiing. That's such an honor, to be recognized for your talent—"

"Shut up!" Laura said. "It's a total fake. There were no dancers at the banquet. This whole thing is a fake! I showed up at the rehearsal and you know who was there? That load Johannsen and his mop. The school was empty. So my mom got on the phone and called the basketball coach, and he knew NOTHING about this letter. He said it had to be a mistake. Well, my mom got completely POed. You know how she gets. So she called Tucci, AT HOME."

"Your mom called the principal! On the weekend?" Valerie said.

"Oh my God!" Michele said.

"She wants answers," Laura said. "And so do I. Tucci said it was a prank. That someone FORGED school stationery and wrote the note as a practical joke."

"Who would do that?" Kaitlin said.

Emma-Jean sat perfectly motionless.

Laura looked over her shoulder at the blacktop. "Take your pick," she said. "There are so many pathetic people who have it out for me."

"Why?" Colleen said.

"They're jealous!" Laura said.

The girls moaned in agreement.

"What a dumb joke," Colleen said.

"It's not a joke! You think this is FUNNY, Colleen?" Laura said.

"No!" Colleen said.

"What if something had happened to me at school? What if I'd been attacked or something? And hello? I missed going skiing."

"That's really horrible," Colleen said.

"Not for you," Laura said. "You got to take my

place, didn't you? You're one of my prime suspects."

Laura narrowed her eyes at Colleen, whose head appeared to sink between her shoulders. "So was it you, Colleen? Did you write that letter? Come on, fess up."

Colleen smiled and made a noise that approximated a laugh, though Emma-Jean thought it sounded more like the whimper of a dog whose tail had been stepped on.

"Colleen would never do that," Kaitlin said.

"No way," said Michele, shaking her head gravely.

"She would never!" said Valerie.

Laura rolled her eyes and then smirked. "Actually I realized you couldn't have because you're a total airhead on the computer."

"I know! I know!" Colleen squeaked. "I totally am!"

"My mother and I just met with Tucci," Laura said. "He said he'd find out who did it."

"That's good," Colleen said.

"No it's not. He's so lame. He won't do anything.

But don't worry. You guys know me. I'll figure this out. And you better believe heads are gonna roll."

Emma-Jean blinked and put her hand up to her neck. Just then the bell rang, signaling the end of lunch period. As the noisy crowd receded, Emma-Jean reflected on what she had just heard. Perhaps Laura had not rebounded quite as quickly from her anger as Emma-Jean had predicted. But she did not believe these recent events would significantly alter the positive outcome of the problem. Emma-Jean did not believe that Laura Gilroy possessed either the reasoning skills or intellectual focus to trace the letter back to its source.

As for Laura's threat to decapitate the responsible party, Emma-Jean was confident she was exaggerating.

Chapter 9

Emma-Jean considered herself fortunate to have so many friends. Her mother was her friend. Her father was her friend, though of course their communion was, by now, purely spiritual. Mr. Johannsen was her friend. Henri was a delightful companion. And there was Vikram, her newest friend, whose arrival six months ago had caused some notable changes in the atmosphere of Stanton Drive.

It had been Emma-Jean's mother's idea to convert the large third floor of their house into a separate apartment. Their house was a bit frayed around the edges, like Emma-Jean's favorite cardigan sweaters. But its rooms were sunny, and unlike many hundred-year-old houses, it smelled good, even on rainy days. The house was just three blocks from the university. Emma-Jean's mother believed, quite justifiably, that they could charge a good rent for the two large rooms and high-ceilinged bathroom on the third floor.

Emma-Jean had written and designed a detailed advertisement, which her mother posted on the bulletin board in the university's housing office. Vikram Adwani had been the first person to call. He had come over one rainy evening for an interview, which had lasted for more than two hours. He made an excellent impression on both Emma-Jean and her mother. He had a serene manner. Judging from his spotless clothing, well-polished boots, and clean fingernails, he practiced excellent hygiene. He maintained a busy schedule of classes and study, which made it unlikely that he would host late-night parties. He moved in three days after their meeting and very quickly assumed responsibility for preparing the evening meal for the entire household.

Within a few weeks of Vikram's arrival, Emma-Jean had moved some school supplies from her desk to the kitchen table, where she would do her home-work. She liked being as close as possible to the won-derful aroma of curry spices and garlic and steam-ing rice, and to Vikram, who hummed in a soft and soothing manner as he chopped and stirred.

Emma-Jean's mother obviously enjoyed the aromas as well. She no longer seemed so exhausted when she returned from her job at the bank. "What are those heavenly smells?" she would say as she hung up her coat. "What delights do you have in store for us today, Vikram?"

Her glasses would fog up as she peeked into the pots of dal or paneer or korma simmering on the stove. Their dinners often stretched for an hour or longer, as they lingered at the table to discuss their days. Vikram would share stories about his stu-dents, which sometimes made her mother laugh. The sound startled Emma-Jean at first, so long had it been since she had heard the carefree and tinkling sound of her mother's merriment.

Sometimes Vikram told about his childhood in the chaotic city of Mumbai, and his words would take

Emma-Jean across two oceans to the shores of the Indian subcontinent. She could vividly imagine the Adwani family's small gated house with the mango tree in the courtyard, the cement floors that cooled one's feet on sultry days, and the sweet-scented jasmine vines that climbed up the walls. It all sounded most pleasant, and Emma-Jean hoped to visit one day.

She also hoped to meet Vikram's mother, who wrote to Vikram every week. Emma-Jean looked forward to finding Mrs. Adwani's letters in the mailbox, the envelopes festooned with brightly colored postage stamps showing famous cricket players and Indian dignitaries wearing high-collared shirts and somber expressions. Emma-Jean was always curious to hear the interesting news of Vikram's family.

The most recent letter contained a picture of a young woman with light brown skin, large, long-lashed brown eyes, and a faint smile.

"Who is this?" Emma-Jean asked.

"This is Jayavanti Prakesh," Vikram said.

"Why did your mother send you her picture? Is she a relative?"

"No," Vikram said. "My mother believes she might be a suitable wife for me."

"Why does she think this?" Emma-Jean said.

Vikram unfolded the letter and read what his mother had written, translating the Hindi into English. ". . . She is from a very good family. Her father is a pulmonary specialist and her mother is a second cousin of your first cousin Prayam's wife, Raya. I had tea with the family and found this girl to be lively and bright, though not stubborn. I do not wish for you to marry a stubborn girl, nor do I wish for you to spend your life with someone who is too meek to express her views. This girl seems not meek and is quite level-headed and very outgoing and talkative. She wishes to be a research biologist, and expounded at great length on her work on cells. So you see you would have much in common."

Vikram handed the letter and picture to Emma-Jean, who studied the Hindi lettering. A few weeks after Vikram moved in, Emma-Jean had begun teaching herself the Hindi alphabet. She had ordered a book at the library and spent long hours studying.

She now knew all of the letters and sounds, and could write them capably. She had even taught Henri the traditional Hindi greeting: *Namaste*.

Emma-Jean examined the photograph of Jaya-vanti Prakesh.

"Have you met this woman?" she asked.

"No," he said. "If I express an interest, my mother will arrange a meeting when I return home for a visit."

"Do you have to marry her?"

"No."

"Do you think she is suitable?"

Vikram studied the picture. "I would need to consider the question over time."

Henri squawked, and Vikram offered him several grains of rice.

"What kind of woman do you want to marry?" Emma-Jean asked.

Vikram went to the refrigerator and took out a glass bowl containing chicken thighs coated in a thick cinnamon-colored marinade. "A strong woman," Vikram said, setting the bowl on the counter. "Someone kind and intelligent and curious, yet also practical.

"I would like to marry somebody I admire," he added, pouring a cup of pearly rice into a pot of water and setting it on the stove. "Someone generous-hearted. Above all, I think, I would like to marry someone with whom I can talk about many things."

A comfortable silence settled over the kitchen and mixed with the sweet smell of simmering basmati rice. Vikram chopped some spinach and onions and set the oven to broil. Emma-Jean sat very still while he worked. It was a good ten minutes before she spoke.

"This woman Jayavanti is not right for you. She would not make you happy."

"How is that?" Vikram asked, raising his thick eyebrows.

"She is talkative and you like it quiet sometimes."

"Yes, that's true."

"And when you are interested in talking, you don't want to talk about science. You like talking about books, or cooking, or India. This woman is a biologist, so she will want to talk to you about science. You will find that tiresome."

Vikram nodded. "Interesting," he said.

It occurred to Emma-Jean that since Vikram's mother was across two oceans, he might need some additional assistance finding a suitable wife. And who better to assist than Emma-Jean, whose problem-solving skills had been honed by her work on behalf of Colleen Pomerantz and Mr. Petrowski? The problem of finding Vikram a suitable wife would not be difficult to solve. Many women would be interested in a man possessing such high intelligence, great cooking talents, and excellent personal hygiene habits.

"Now that you have told me the kind of woman you are looking for, I will try to find you the person you should marry."

"Really?" Vikram said, raising his eyebrows even higher.

"Yes," Emma-Jean replied.

"I look forward to your thoughts on the matter," Vikram said.

Chapter 10

Did Emma-Jean Lazarus write the letter to Laura Gilroy?

Colleen shook her head and tried to focus on her math quiz.

Oh gosh. What if Emma-Jean wrote it?

Colleen pressed down so hard with her pencil that the point broke and flew up over her shoulder. She fished another pencil out of her backpack and took a deep breath.

No, of course Emma-Jean hadn't written the letter. That would be just too weird.

Colleen stared at the algebra equations. She had gotten all the practice questions right last night. But now the numbers seemed to be buzzing all around on the paper, like a swarm of wasps.

Emma-Jean did it!

No she didn't.

Colleen closed her eyes and *ordered* this idea to *please* leave her brain. But it kept sneaking in through some secret door in Colleen's skull.

Finally Colleen realized she had to do something or her head would explode. Somehow she managed to finish the quiz. Then she wrote a note and snuck it into Emma-Jean's locker while everyone was at lunch.

Dear Emma-Jean,

Hi! How are you? I hope the answer to that question is GREAT!

Can I talk to you today? I have to talk to you about Laura Gilroy and the ski trip. If you are free, you can meet me on the benches on the far side of the soccer field. I'll wait until 3:10. Don't worry if you can't make it. I have nothing to do after school anyway, so no sweat!

Have a great day! Colleen P.

Colleen could see Emma-Jean coming across the soccer field. She reminded herself to be calm. She'd just ask Emma-Jean if she'd written the letter and Emma-Jean would say, "Of course not, silly!" or something Emma-Jean-ish that meant the same thing. Everything would be fine, Colleen told herself.

"Hi, Emma-Jean!" Colleen said in a voice she wanted to sound normal but sounded totally desperate.

Emma-Jean nodded and pointed at Colleen's cheek.

"What is that?"

"What?" Colleen said, her hands flying to her face. Did she have a blob of lotion on her cheek or something even grosser?

"That sparkling substance," Emma-Jean said. "On your cheek. Does it cause your skin to itch?"

"Oh!" Colleen had to smile. "Emma-Jean, it's just makeup! You don't even know it's on! Hey . . ."

Colleen reached into her backpack and pulled out

her purple makeup pouch, which Valerie had brought her back from Disney World. Her little tub of sparkly powder was right on top. She opened it and held it out to Emma-Jean.

"Try some," Colleen said. "You'd look so pretty with some makeup—oh! No offense! I don't mean that you're not pretty now! Really, you're gorgeous! But makeup can enhance your features." Colleen's mom didn't like her wearing too much makeup, but Colleen would never go out without at least some lip gloss and a little blush.

Emma-Jean shook her head. "I don't care for that at all."

"Really?" Did Emma-Jean mean that she didn't like Colleen's own sparkling cheeks? That Colleen looked bad?

No, she told herself. Remember that Emma-Jean isn't like other people who say mean things to be funny or to make you feel bad. Emma-Jean just says exactly what she thinks, which is really good because then a person doesn't have to spend hours—days—wondering if she actually meant something else. Emma-Jean said she didn't like the sparkling makeup. She did not say Colleen looked bad. So see? There was no reason to feel worried.

Which was a relief.

"Anyway," Colleen said, putting her powder away and getting down to business. "The reason I wanted to meet is . . . did you do something to Laura Gilroy?"

"What do you mean by do something?"

"I don't know, I just wondered, after we talked in the bathroom that day, and I told you about the problem with Laura and Kaitlin . . . you didn't do anything, did you?"

"Yes, I did."

Colleen blinked.

"What did you do?" Colleen said, trying to keep her voice steady.

"I wrote the letter to Laura. The one she showed you the other day. On the blacktop."

"On no . . . oh . . . oh my gosh," Colleen said, easing herself down onto the grass. She hoped she wouldn't throw up, like she did after getting off the Tilt-A-Whirl at last year's Pumpkin Festival, which had been one of the top ten humiliations of Colleen's entire life.

"You wrote that?"

"Yes."

Colleen had suspected it. So why was she so stunned?

Because Colleen was always thinking and worrying and obsessing about things. That she'd failed the social studies quiz or that her new jeans made her look huge or that her breath smelled like egg salad. And part of the worrying and obsessing was secretly knowing that really she was wrong, that she'd gotten an A on the quiz and that her jeans looked okay and that her breath smelled minty and everything would turn out fine.

Except for this time.

"Oh, Emma-Jean, why did you do that?"

"Because you said you wanted my help," Emma-Jean said.

"Oh, well, I didn't exactly realize that you were

going to, you know, do something. Like this."

"The letter was successful," Emma-Jean said. "You went skiing."

"Well, yes, I guess. But now . . . what if Laura figures it out? What if she figures out you wrote it . . . for me? Because I think she knows something. She thinks I had something to do with it. Because Laura's acting really mean. I mean meaner than usual. I hope you know that if Laura finds out, she's going to think I told you to do it, and she'll be really, really mad. And Emma-Jean, she can be so awful—if she finds out I had anything to do with it, she'll . . ."

Colleen closed her eyes to stop herself from thinking about the horrible things Laura might do to her.

"I will not tell her," Emma-Jean said.

"I know!" Colleen said. "I know you totally wouldn't. But she's smarter than she looks, and I'm worried she could figure it out."

"I think it's unlikely," Emma-Jean said.

Colleen nodded. Her body had turned to Jell-O. She wished she could recapture the feeling she'd had the other day at school, when for just a few moments she really didn't care what Laura Gilroy thought of her.

But that had lasted no longer than the flavor in a stick of sugarless bubble gum. And now Colleen felt terrified. She might as well leave the state. Did the witness protection program accept thirteen-year-olds?

Colleen stood up, but she was all wobbly, and Emma-Jean reached out and grabbed her arm. Colleen bit her lip so hard, she tasted blood through her fruity lip gloss. Was she going into shock?

Emma-Jean was staring at her again. Why did she do that?

"May I ask you a question?" Emma-Jean said.

Colleen nodded.

"Why are you afraid of Laura Gilroy?"

Colleen tried to laugh, but no sound came out. "I'm not afraid of her."

"Yes you are," Emma-Jean said. "Even the mention of Laura Gilroy's name causes you to flinch and avert your eyes."

"It's not that I'm afraid. It's just that Laura can be . . . so mean."

"But she cannot hurt you."

"Yes she can, Emma-Jean. She totally can."

"How? Laura Gilroy is not a physically violent person."

"You wouldn't understand," Colleen said. "She . . ."

How could Colleen explain how it was with girls like Laura—girls who never told you your haircut looked pretty or your new shoes were cool, who never held out a bag of potato chips and said, "Take as many as you want," who with one look could make you feel like the tiniest bug, or worse, a bug nobody could see.

How could a girl like that make everyone want to be her friend?

Come to think of it, Colleen didn't understand it either. It just *was*.

Colleen stared at the grass and shook her head. "I don't know," she said. "I really don't."

"Do you know anything about chimpanzees?" Emma-Jean said.

"What?" Colleen said.

"Chimps are very much like humans. In their

communities, certain individuals become dominant. These individuals are known as the alpha chimps. They achieve dominance through intimidation. They bare their teeth and beat their chests and achieve control of the group because the others feel threatened."

"That's really interesting, Emma-Jean. But why are you telling me this?"

"Because you think Laura Gilroy is the alpha chimp."

"But we're not chimps. We're people."

"Exactly," Emma-Jean said. "We are not chimps and thus we possess the mental capacity to understand that while Laura Gilroy might behave in a menacing fashion, she cannot cause real harm because we are humans who live in a civilized human society. We are not chimps in the jungle."

Colleen's heart was racing. She could not focus on what Emma-Jean was saying. Why was she talking about chimps when Colleen's life was ruined?

This was a mess. A huge, horrible mess. She needed to get home. Her mother would be waiting for her and would not be happy that Colleen was late. She and her mom were going to stores to collect donations for a church youth group project Colleen had organized. Just because her life was ruined didn't mean she could forget her responsibilities to the homeless families depending on her. Really, her own problems were so tiny and stupid compared to what so many other people dealt with. People like Emma-Jean, who had lost her dad. Colleen knew all this. She really knew it! So why did her own problems seem so gigantic?

She wanted to cry, but she flashed a smile for Emma-Jean, who was just trying to help her, right? She couldn't be mad at Emma-Jean, because poor Emma-Jean didn't understand anything about anything.

Chapter 11

The next afternoon, Emma-Jean was about to leave through the side door of the William Gladstone building when Mr. Petrowski's voice caught her attention. He was speaking in an angry tone, and Emma-Jean sensed that there was a matter requiring her attention. She followed the sound of his voice until she came to its source. Her instinct had been correct. Mr. Petrowski was standing in the doorway of the gym. He was yelling at Will Keeler.

Emma-Jean stood back so they wouldn't see her, though she could see Mr. Petrowski's jowly profile.

"You think rules don't apply to you, don't you?" Mr. Petrowski was saying.

"That's not true, sir," said Will Keeler, who was as tall as Mr. Petrowski. "I don't know why you think that—"

"Well, for that little stunt today I'm taking twenty points off your final grade. Take that to the bank."

"Mr. Petrowski, that wasn't me! I didn't write that! That's totally unfair. If you take twenty points off my grade, I'll get, like . . ."

"According to my calculations, that would take your grade down to a, let's see . . . sixty-one . . . D minus."

"You can't do that! My parents will kill me! They won't let me go to basketball camp over spring break! This is totally unfair!"

"Unfair?" Mr. Petrowski said with an unkind smirk on his face. "Maybe it is. But you know what? There's nothing you can do about it."

Mr. Petrowski turned and stormed off. Will Keeler remained hidden in the doorway. Emma-Jean stood very still and quiet, quiet enough to hear the soft sniffling noises coming from where Will was standing.

She came up behind Will, who was facing the wall.

"Can I help you?" Emma-Jean said.

He whirled around, glaring at first. But then his face drooped.

"Oh," he muttered. "Emma-Jean."

"I'm sorry you are distressed."

"Petrowski said I drew a picture of him on the board, a fat guy with the name Mr. Pigtrowski. It's ridiculous. First of all, I would never do anything so lame. And B, I can't draw at all."

"I know that. I sat across from you in art last quarter."

"You did?

"Yes, I did."

"Okay," he said. "Well, I gotta go, so . . ."

"I believe I know why you are having troubles with Mr. Petrowski," she said.

"What are you talking about?" Will said.

"I heard him speaking to Ms. Wright in the cafeteria. He suspected you in the theft of some candy from his locker."

"What the . . ."

"Some of his chocolates were missing, and he observed you eating chocolate in science class."

"Someone put that chocolate in my backpack! I swear! I ate one and it tasted like garbage, so I gave the whole box away."

"I was able to exonerate you. Mr. Petrowski now knows the truth: The thief was a mouse. However, it is obvious to me that Mr. Petrowski continues to harbor very negative feelings toward you."

"What did I do to him?" Will said.

"You did nothing," Emma-Jean assured him. "I think this relates to a problem Mr. Petrowski is having with his Cadillac Escalade. I heard him complaining to Ms. Wright about the poor service he is getting at Keeler Cadillac."

"What are you talking about? What does that have to do with me?"

"Maybe you should speak to your father about rectifying the situation."

"My dad has nothing to do with that place. He's a landscaper. It's my uncle who owns it, and my uncle's a jerk. He doesn't care about anything but money. Him and my dad don't even talk to each other. I never see my uncle, except on those stupid billboards."

"That is unfortunate," Emma-Jean said.

She studied Will for a moment. His eyes were a striking color, the very same light blue as the cover of the *Oxford English Dictionary*. She imagined him, for a fleeting second, riding a white horse.

"Okay," Will said, stepping into the hallway. "I'll see you."

"If you would like, I could attempt to help you solve this problem."

"Are you kidding me?"

"I am most serious."

Will Keeler laughed. "That's a good one," he said. "Really good." He took Emma-Jean by the shoulders and moved her to the side. Normally, Emma-Jean disliked being touched by people she didn't know very well. However, Will Keeler was gentle. The feeling of his hands on her shoulders was not unpleasant.

"Who are you, Nancy freakin' Drew?"

"Excuse me?" Emma-Jean said.

Will Keeler shook his head and jogged away. "Nancy freakin' Drew!" His laughter echoed through the hallways.

Later that same afternoon, Colleen and Kaitlin were on the playground of the St. Mary's Catholic Church, waiting for Colleen's mom to pick them up. The church youth group had worked for hours putting together toiletry kits for people in homeless shelters. Being homeless didn't mean you didn't care about how you looked, did it? When they had finished, Father William had hugged Colleen and told her how proud he was of all of them.

Colleen had smiled. She'd felt happy and safe in the church. But now, out here in the open, she felt scared again. Even the wind seemed to be whispering to her, trying to warn her about something terrible.

All day, Laura Gilroy had been acting mean. And not the usual ignoring mean. In language arts, while Ms. Wright was talking about *To Kill a Mockingbird*,

Laura Gilroy was staring at Colleen. Colleen smiled and waved, but Laura just kept on staring like her eyes were lasers and she wanted to burn two holes in Colleen's forehead. And now Kaitlin was telling her that Laura had been talking about Colleen during health class.

"She asked about our ski trip and if we had a good time."

Colleen nodded.

"She asked if you said anything about tricking her so she wouldn't go."

"That's paranoid," Colleen said, trying to sound nonchalant, which wasn't easy because how could you act like you didn't care about something when you cared about every single little tiny miniscule thing?

She was dying to tell Kaitlin the truth about Emma-Jean and the letter. Kaitlin would understand. They'd had so much fun together singing on the chair lift and skiing after that cute snowboarding guy and pretending they were in Switzerland and painting their toenails alternating colors of bright red and light pink. She knew Kaitlin would never tell her secret, or if she did, there would have to be a really good reason, like someone was threatening to hurt Monty, Kaitlin's cat.

But she didn't want Emma-Jean to get in trouble. And wasn't it really *weird* that she'd confided in Emma-Jean? Didn't it mean that she was sort of desperate?

"She is paranoid," said Kaitlin, inching her swing closer to Colleen's so that their shoulders touched. "Then she started asking me if you'd taken any computer classes lately."

Colleen's heart popped out of her body and landed in the sand in front of the swings, where it sank through all the layers of the earth and fell out the bottom into space.

"Why did she ask that?" she said in a whispery voice that sounded like the total opposite of nonchalant.

"I don't know. No offense, but I reminded her that computers weren't really your thing."

"Then what did she say?"

"That was it."

"Why is she so interested in me all of a sudden?" Colleen said. "She never seemed to care so much before."

"Maybe she's jealous of you because you're so pretty," Kaitlin said, which Colleen thought was a really, really supportive thing to say even though it wasn't true and Kaitlin knew it.

"This is all my fault," Kaitlin said, her voice a little shaky. "I should never have invited her. Why did I do that?"

"Don't beat yourself up!" Colleen said. "She has this power. She's like . . . the queen chimp."

"What?" Kaitlin gave her a strange look.

"You know," Colleen said, "she just makes you feel like you have to do what she wants."

"I bet she's jealous because she knows we're best friends." Kaitlin put her head on Colleen's shoulder.

"Yeah," Colleen said.

They sat like that a while until somehow Colleen's heart came back from space and pushed its way through all the layers of the earth and back into her chest.

Chapter 12

It was true that Will Keeler had not asked Emma-Jean to work on his problem. But that didn't mean that Emma-Jean should rule out the idea of assisting him. He had a serious problem. And Emma-Jean had every reason to believe that she could solve it for him.

There were subtle indications that he wanted help. He had laughed at the end of their meeting, which suggested that her offer to help him had made him happy. He had referred to her as Nancy Drew. Being compared to Nancy Drew was flattering. Perhaps Will had sensed somehow that Emma-Jean's superior observational and analytical powers were on par with those of the legendary fictional detective.

In any case, Will Keeler never said he *didn't* want her assistance, and he could not rationally object if she took it upon herself to help him. Certainly if the outcome was positive, Will Keeler would be pleased. And if she was unsuccessful, he would never have to know that she had tried.

Emma-Jean decided that she would move forward.

She sat at her tidy desk, a spiral notebook open in front of her, and focused her thoughts. Was Mr. Petrowski consciously punishing Will Keeler for the wrongs committed by the owners of Keeler Cadillac? Emma-Jean hoped not. She hated to think that any member of the William Gladstone staff would behave in such a way. No. Mr. Petrowski had been driven— quite literally—out of the bounds of rational thinking by his problems with the car dealership. And in this irrational state of mind, he had convinced himself that Will Keeler was a person capable of stealing candy and drawing vulgar pictures.

The essence of the problem was clear: In order

to solve Will Keeler's problem, Emma-Jean had to solve Mr. Petrowski's problem, which of course had nothing at all to do with Will Keeler.

Emma-Jean devised a strategy.

She relocated to her computer desk and found the Cadillac Web site. She searched the company directory of senior executives until she found the Director of Worldwide Customer Service, whose name was Kevin Kelly. She imported the Cadillac logo into a Quark document and turned it into a piece of authentic-looking Cadillac stationery.

She then composed a stern letter to Keeler Cadillac instructing them to make immediate amends to a valued customer named Phil Petrowski. She recalled what Will had told her about his uncle— that he cared only for money—and crafted her message accordingly.

. . . . Those of us at worldwide headquarters will not stand for any dealer who jeopardizes our reputation as leaders in automotive quality and customer service. We will seek monetary damages if the matter of Phil Petrowski is not resolved immediately.

She finished the letter, read it over twice, and signed Kevin Kelly's name in her most masculine and authoritative cursive.

She created a Cadillac envelope and found the address of Keeler Cadillac in the Riverview phonebook. By 5:00, she had mailed the letter and was enjoying a cup of tea and an apple, with Henri dozing peacefully on her shoulder.

Chapter 13

Though Emma-Jean had been extremely busy as of late, she had not forgotten her plan to find a wife for Vikram Adwani. In fact, Emma-Jean already had a possible candidate in her sights.

During lunch period, Emma-Jean lingered in the seventh-grade hallway outside Ms. Wright's room. Unless she had cafeteria duty, Ms. Wright spent her lunch period alone in her classroom, reading and eating a sandwich she brought from home.

Emma-Jean had already determined that her favorite teacher had many qualities that would make her a suitable match for Vikram Adwani. Like

Vikram, Ms. Wright enjoyed solitude and quiet. She loved to read, and every two to three days arrived at school with a different novel from the library poking out of her large woven shoulder bag. She was immaculately clean and organized. Her commanding way with unruly seventh graders suggested she possessed the kind of strength Vikram was looking for.

Emma-Jean now intended to find out if Ms. Wright would be able to satisfy two of Vikram's requirements: that his future wife be able to converse with him on a wide range of topics, and that she like Indian food. Vikram hadn't specifically mentioned that a taste for curry was a requirement. It was simply appropriate that whoever married Vikram Adwani should appreciate the delicious meals he prepared.

Emma-Jean knocked on the doorframe to announce herself. Ms. Wright smiled and motioned for Emma-Jean to come in.

"Did you have a question about class?" she asked, tossing the crusts of her sandwich into a brown paper bag and brushing her hands together. "I just finished grading your essay about Robert Frost's poem. It was a lovely piece of work, I think."

"Thank you," Emma-Jean said.

"You obviously appreciate Robert Frost."

"Robert Frost was an excellent poet," Emma-Jean said. It had been easy to write about him. His observations about winter in New Hampshire made Emma-Jean feel that she and Mr. Frost shared the same pair of eyes.

"I like him too," Ms. Wright said.

"Do you like poetry in general?" Emma-Jean asked, believing that somebody interested in poetry would likely have far-ranging interests.

"I like many types of poetry," said Ms. Wright. "I'm introducing myself to more and more modern poets." She reached into her bag and pulled out a paperback book. "This is Mary Oliver's collection. Would you like to borrow it?"

Emma-Jean shook her head. She was too busy at the moment. If Ms. Wright married Vikram Adwani, Emma-Jean would find the time to borrow her poetry books. She was hopeful that the young couple would live in Vikram's third-floor apartment. That would make the borrowing of books highly convenient for Emma-Jean.

Emma-Jean reached into her briefcase and pulled out her thermos. It was not filled with soup today. It was filled with curried chicken and lentils. She'd also brought an extra spoon and paper cup. She unscrewed the top, planning to offer Ms. Wright a sample. But before she could, her teacher gasped and said, "Is that curry I smell? Oh, that is my absolute favorite! You know, I traveled in India for a year after college and I just love the food . . ."

Ms. Wright went on, but Emma-Jean was no longer listening. She had no doubt that she had found a more than suitable wife for Vikram Adwani. There was just one last thing she had to determine, a rather delicate matter.

"My friend Vikram Adwani cooks this food. Perhaps you'd like to come to dinner. You could bring your boyfriend if you like . . ."

"Oh, well, I'd love to come, but I don't have a boy-friend."

"That will be fine. You should come by yourself. I will follow up with some possible dates."

Walking home, Emma-Jean imagined what she might wear to the Adwani/Wright nuptials. Perhaps she would wear a sari.

Chapter 14

The following Tuesday, Colleen Pomerantz was changing for gym class in the girls' locker room. As usual, she stalled until the other girls were in the gym. Colleen had the worst cellulite in America and didn't like changing in front of people. She had folded her clothes and put them in her locker when she heard footsteps. She grabbed her gym shorts, but before she could put them on Laura Gilroy appeared. She stood between the rows of lockers, cornering Colleen like a chipmunk. A chipmunk with cellulite.

"Well, hi," Laura said, folding her arms across her chest and leaning her shoulder against a locker.

"Hi, Laura," Colleen said. Somehow she put on

her gym shorts, which wasn't easy because her legs were shaking.

"Nervous?"

Colleen closed her eyes and shook her head.

In nightmares, sometimes Colleen would close her eyes and think really hard, *This is just a nightmare,* and when she opened her eyes the killer lunatic maniac with the bloody axe would go *poof* and Colleen would be back in her happy pink room with her flowered rug and Hello Kitty clock ticking softly. But now when she opened her eyes, Laura Gilroy was still standing there staring at her. Colleen would rather have the maniac. At least he'd kill her quickly, chop her head right off. Laura would definitely torture her first.

"I know exactly what's going on," Laura said in a scary cool voice. "I know you asked Emma-Jean Lazarus to write that letter because you were so peeved about me going skiing with Kaitlin. I figured it out, because I'm not an IDIOT. So you might as well admit it to me now, because you are both going to be in huge trouble. You might even get expelled."

How did she know for sure? Did Emma-Jean tell?

No, that was impossible.

Colleen opened her mouth but couldn't talk because her tongue was stuck and she couldn't look away from Laura because her eyeballs were cemented in place. She was a rock. It was like in that Greek myth Ms. Wright read to them, where that lady with live snakes for hair—Madonna? No, Medusa!—she would look at you and if you looked at her in the eyes, she was so horrible and evil, you would turn to stone.

Laura was like Medusa! She had turned Colleen into a statue!

"I knew it had to be you," Laura/Medusa hissed. "You're so lame, Colleen, to stoop so low, with Emma-Jean Lazarus."

There was a knock on the locker room door.

"Hello? Hello?"

Mr. Johannsen.

"Anyone in here? I hear there's a toilet on the fritz!"

Colleen sprang to her feet, freed by the sound of the nice custodian's voice.

"You're so lucky," Laura murmured, heading toward the exit. She threw her shoulder against the door and stepped out.

"Careful there, young lady!" Mr. Johannsen said, but too late. Laura tripped over the edge of his bucket, and brown soapy water sloshed onto the floor, soaking one of Laura's spanking-new sneakers.

"Why don't you watch where you put that thing!" she cried, bending down to inspect her foot.

"You all right there, missy?" he said. "I've got some paper towels right here."

"My shoe is totally RUINED!" said Laura, fluttering her eyes. "You should pay for this!"

"Sorry, Mr. Johannsen," Colleen whispered, scurrying away from Laura.

She had escaped, for now.

But there would be a next time, and Colleen knew she wouldn't be so lucky.

Chapter 15

The night before their dinner with Ms. Wright, Vikram and Emma-Jean sat at the kitchen table discussing Vikram's menu ideas. Emma-Jean had not informed Vikram that the guest was very likely to become his wife. He simply knew that their guest was a teacher Emma-Jean admired, and that a festive meal was called for. He was describing to Emma-Jean one of his mother's signature dishes, a stuffed bread called puran-poli, when his phone rang.

Emma-Jean assumed it was one of his students, who often called in the evenings with questions about office hours and assignments. But then Vikram began speaking very quickly in Hindi. Emma-Jean had to wait until he had hung up the phone to learn that the caller had been his sister, Shefali.

"My mother is very ill," Vikram explained. His voice sounded different, as though he had burned his throat on very hot tea. "She has experienced a heart attack. She is now in the hospital, in intensive care. I must fly to Mumbai immediately."

A frenzy of activity swept the household. Emma-Jean's mother got on the phone to make Vikram's plane reservations and Vikram packed. Emma-Jean joined him in his room. As Vikram tossed clothes onto the bed, Emma-Jean folded them neatly and put them into his worn red leather suitcase. She carefully sealed his toothpaste and shampoo into Ziploc bags and packed those as well.

"Thank you for helping me," he said.

"How long will you be gone?" Emma-Jean said.

"I don't know," he said. "I cannot think clearly right now. I have been seized by a painfully irrational thought."

"What is that?"

"That I broke my mother's heart."

"I don't understand."

"I broke her heart by leaving India and coming here. By not marrying."

"You told us your mother urged you to come here. You said it was her dream that you become a professor at a great university."

"That is true," he said. "I told you I am not thinking clearly. Right now I think my own heart is breaking at the thought of my mother suffering."

"Your mother has a very strong heart," Emma-Jean said.

"How do you know?" Vikram said. "You have not met her."

"It is obvious. Because only a woman with a good heart could have raised a person of your excellent character."

Vikram looked at Emma-Jean and nodded, and then quickly looked down at his suitcase. "Thank you, Emma-Jean," he said softly.

Emma-Jean's mother said that of course she and Emma-Jean would take him to the airport to catch his midnight flight. Emma-Jean felt uneasy about Vikram being by himself during this crisis, away from her and her mother. What if he became distressed during the flight? What would he do for comfort?

Emma-Jean rushed up to her room and took her father's quilt off her bed. She held the soft cotton up to her face, breathing in its deeply familiar smell. She hesitated for only a moment before folding it up into a neat rectangle and rushing it down the stairs. She tucked it into the Pittsburgh Steelers duffel that Vikram had packed to carry onto the plane, satisfied that it would bring him as much comfort as it had brought her during those long and difficult nights over two years ago.

It took them under an hour to get to the airport. They found the Air India terminal, and Emma-Jean's mother pulled up next to the curb. She and Emma-Jean got out and stood with Vikram as he checked his pockets for his passport and travel documents. Through the window, Emma-Jean could see many people lined up at the ticket window. Many of the women were dressed in orange and red and yellow, which brightened the grim and dark night.

"I wish you the best, my friend," said Vikram to Emma-Jean. "I will call as soon as I can."

He turned and looked at Emma-Jean's mother.

"I'll miss our talks."

"I will too," her mother said. "We will be thinking of you all the time." She leaned over and hugged Vikram, who wrapped his arms tightly around her mother's narrow shoulders. It was some time before they stepped away from each other.

Emma-Jean stared at her mother and then at Vikram. Suddenly, in a burst of light, Emma-Jean saw a possible future. It was as though, for an instant, the night had turned itself inside out to reveal new and unsettling possibilities.

Emma-Jean and her mother stood close together on the curb as Vikram walked through the automatic doors and was swallowed by the brightly colored crowd. They shivered in their parkas, but neither moved until a bus pulled up and the driver shouted for Emma-Jean's mother to move the car.

After they got home, Emma-Jean's mother kissed Emma-Jean good night and went up to bed. Emma-Jean went to the kitchen and looked up Ms. Wright's phone number in the William Gladstone Middle School Directory. She left a message informing Ms. Wright of an unforeseen crisis in Vikram's family, and that the dinner would have to be postponed indefinitely.

She hung up the phone and stood for several minutes in front of the picture of her father on the refrigerator. The kitchen held the lingering aroma of curry and garlic, which made Emma-Jean miss Vikram even more. However, she told herself that it was best that her friend had gone.

There could be only one love of Emma-Jean's mother's life, and that was Eugene Lazarus.

Chapter 16

Emma-Jean was about to leave the William Gladstone building on Friday afternoon when Will Keeler stopped her at the door.

"Hey," he said softly, his bright eyes darting up and down the hallway. The buses had departed but students were still in the building for extra help and chorus practice. Will motioned for Emma-Jean to follow him, and led her upstairs to the foreign language wing, which was deserted.

"So, uh, did you do something?" he said.

"What do you mean precisely?" Emma-Jean said.

"I mean, did you do something to get Petrowski to leave me alone?"

"I did take some action designed to help you with your problem."

Will Keeler's smooth, angular face broke into a smile.

"Nancy freakin' Drew."

He reached into his back pocket and pulled out a crumpled slip of paper. "Petrowski gave out the third-quarter grades today."

"I know," Emma-Jean said. Her average was, as usual, 100 percent.

He pushed the paper into her hands.

"Look at this! Eighty-one! He didn't take the points off! I got my B minus! B minus, baby!"

Will Keeler pumped his fist in the air, a gesture of triumph.

"What did you do?" Will said. "I gotta hear this."

"I prefer not to discuss the details and am pleased you are satisfied with the outcome."

"Hey, I'm pleased. I'm gonna wet my pants, I'm so happy!"

Emma-Jean stepped back in alarm, but Will

Keeler leaned close to her, so close that she could smell the coppery scent of his skin.

"Listen, Emma-Jean. I owe you one. Big time."

"You owe me nothing."

Only an unscrupulous person would accept payment for solving a problem.

Will Keeler put his hand on Emma-Jean's head and ruffled her hair.

"You're really okay, Emma-Jean. I mean, you're a good kid."

After Will had gone, Emma-Jean took a walk through the William Gladstone parking lot. She knew where all the teachers customarily parked. She stopped in front of Mr. Petrowski's parking space and noted with satisfaction the brand-new cherry red Cadillac Escalade. Emma-Jean shook her head. People really weren't so complex after all.

As she walked home, Emma-Jean had the feeling that Will Keeler's hand was still resting on her head. It was a most pleasant sensation.

Chapter 17

Emma-Jean and Henri were enjoying a quiet afternoon in Emma-Jean's room when the doorbell startled them both.

Emma-Jean left Henri in her room and went to investigate. She opened the door and saw perhaps the very last person she would expect to see on her porch: Laura Gilroy.

"Hi," Laura said. "I was in the neighborhood. Mind if I come in?"

"Yes," Emma-Jean said. "I am not permitted to have visitors while my mother is at work."

Laura raised an eyebrow. "Oh come on, Emma-

Jean. I wanted to say hi. Didn't you know? I stop by my friends' houses all the time."

"But we are not friends," Emma-Jean said. Emma-Jean would never associate closely with a girl of Laura's unscrupulous character.

"Oh," Laura said, walking through the doorway past Emma-Jean. "You're hilarious."

Hilarious was not a word that Emma-Jean would use to describe herself, even when she was in a mirthful mood.

"No, I—"

"Interesting house," Laura interrupted, surveying the living room. "My mom just paid a total fortune for a rug like that."

"My parents brought that home from Turkey," Emma-Jean said. "They went there on their honeymoon."

"I bet your room's really cool too," Laura said, heading toward the stairs. "It's up here, right?"

Before Emma-Jean could answer, Laura was rushing up the steep, narrow staircase, her black parka billowing behind her in a most sinister manner.

Emma-Jean rushed after her, taking the stairs two at a time. She found Laura in her room, standing at her desk.

"I'll repeat what I said to you downstairs," Emma-Jean said, out of breath from her sprint up the stairs. "I am not allowed to have visitors now."

Laura opened her mouth as if to speak, but then was overcome by a violent fit of coughing. Her face turned bright red and she pounded her chest.

"A drink," Laura sputtered, hands at her throat. "Juice. Cold. Please hurry!"

Emma-Jean hesitated. She did not want to leave Laura Gilroy alone in her room. However, she could not simply allow her to choke, possibly to death.

Emma-Jean rushed down the stairs. She would get some juice. Once she was sure Laura's airway was clear, she would ask her—firmly—to leave.

And if she refused? Emma-Jean wasn't sure what action to take.

Perhaps she would have to call the police.

Fortunately, this was not necessary. As Emma-Jean was leaving the kitchen with a tall glass of cold grape juice, a piercing shriek rang through the house. Laura Gilroy raced down the stairs, shouting, "Get it off me! Get it off me!"

Before Emma-Jean could respond, Laura was gone.

Emma-Jean stood in the hallway. She was perplexed, until she saw, perched on the banister, Henri. The bird flew down and settled on Emma-Jean's shoulder.

"Emma-Jean," the bird squawked. "Emma-Jean."

"Thank you, Henri," she said, gently rubbing a finger against the back of Henri's tiny head. "As I've told you before, you are a very perceptive creature."

That night, Emma-Jean and her mother ate dinner together at the kitchen table. Her mother made what was once Emma-Jean's favorite evening meal: broiled chicken and broccoli. Emma-Jean complimented her mother on the chicken, which was crisp yet moist. But after months of curry and chutneys and daals, the chicken tasted almost unbearably bland. Emma-Jean was about to tell her about her most unpleasant encounter with Laura Gilroy, when the phone rang. Her mother reached over and grabbed the phone from the counter.

"Oh, Vikram!" her mother said, standing up so abruptly that her napkin fell onto the floor. "Hello! How are you! We've been thinking of you!"

Emma-Jean's eyes followed her mother as she paced excitedly around their kitchen with the phone pressed to her ear. "Oh wonderful! Yes! Fantastic! I can't tell you how happy I am to hear that." She smiled at Emma-Jean and nodded. "Yes! Yes! I got your e-mails. We miss you too. Yes . . ."

She glanced at Emma-Jean and then walked out of the kitchen. Emma-Jean heard the front door squeak and her mother's footsteps on the porch. Emma-Jean frowned. It was thirty-three degrees outside.

It was several minutes before her mother returned to the table. Her cheeks were pink and her eyes sparkled as though her lashes had turned to tiny icicles.

"Vikram's mother is going to be fine!" she said.

"That is very good," Emma-Jean said.

"I miss him. Don't you? It feels a bit . . . I don't

know, lonely here without him. Don't you think?"

"I'm not lonely when you are here."

"Well of course I'm not lonely with you either, I'm just saying that it's a little different, don't you think?"

Emma-Jean nodded, but she was already contemplating this unsettling problem. It was clear that Vikram's absence had in no way loosened the bond between him and her mother.

"Tomorrow night I think we should go out to dinner," her mother said. "To that Indian restaurant." She got up and began clearing the dishes. "That's exactly what we should do." She hummed as they did the dishes and prepared a cup of Vikram's favorite chai tea to take up to her room. Emma-Jean watched her closely, with growing alarm.

After they'd said good night, Emma-Jean sat down at her computer, gripped by a grim sense of purpose. She missed her friend Vikram, but it was necessary that she take action to ensure that he stayed in India, away from her mother, who already had a love of her life. This was deeply regrettable, since Vikram was one of Emma-Jean's closest friends. But there was no alternative.

It was well past midnight when she finally settled on a strategy. It was a risky plan. But as Poincaré once wrote, delicate problems require creative solutions. With the Frenchman's words in her mind, Emma-Jean turned on her computer and wrote the following letter.

Dear Mrs. Adwani,

I am writing to tell you that your son Vikram is in love with my mother, Elizabeth Lazarus. It is understandable that Vikram would be in love with my mother, since she is a highly intelligent and sensitive person. It is also understandable that Elizabeth Lazarus would feel affection toward your son, since he possesses a fine character, is a talented cook, and practices excellent personal hygiene. Under normal circumstances, he would make an excellent husband for Elizabeth Lazarus. However, Elizabeth Lazarus is already in love with another man. His name is Eugene Lazarus. He was a brilliant mathematics professor. Though he died over two years ago, he remains the love of Elizabeth Lazarus's life. You can understand that it is not possible for her to be in love with another man.

I felt it was necessary to inform you of this situation since it is your responsibility to find a suitable wife for your son. I suggest you expedite your efforts to find a woman who meets Vikram's specifications. If you would like my ideas on this subject, you may contact me at any time.

Congratulations on recovering from your heart attack. Now you must watch your diet carefully to prevent further arterial blockage. Also, exercise is an important part of your recovery program. I recommend a brisk thirty-minute walk each day. I understand from my reading that Mumbai is a crowded city with a serious traffic problem. I recommend that you find a safe place to conduct your daily walk.

Sincerely,
Emma-Jean Lazarus

Emma-Jean addressed the envelope. For added credibility, she wrote her name and return address in Hindi lettering.

Chapter 18

Colleen was about to leave school at the end of the day when she felt a clawlike grip on her shoulder.

"Come," said Laura Gilroy.

Laura took Colleen's arm and led her—dragged her, basically—through the empty halls of William Gladstone. They wound up at the girls' locker room. Laura pushed the door open and gave Colleen a little shove.

"Sit," she said, pointing to the changing bench.

Colleen sat.

"It's over," Laura said. "For you and Emma-Jean Lazarus. I have proof."

Colleen opened her mouth to talk. No sound came out.

"Emma-Jean Lazarus keeps files in her room. You should see. All these files about weird stuff like germs and trees. And she had this one file that was so interesting. You know what the file was called?" Laura opened her eyes wide and flashed her straight white teeth like a vampire. "Colleen Pomerantz!"

Colleen looked at her sneakers, which looked very small and helpless, like kittens that had just been born.

"You know what's in the file? A copy of that bogus letter I got, about the basketball banquet. And you know what else? A note that you wrote, on your lame heart stationery, telling Emma-Jean you need to talk to her about . . . let me remember exactly . . . oh, right—Laura Gilroy and the ski trip. What do you think of that?"

Colleen had no thoughts. Her brain had melted.

"It all adds up," Laura said. "And tomorrow morning, I'm going to take that file from my locker, and bring it straight to Tucci. And then . . . well, we'll see what happens. But it won't be good. For you or that freak Emma-Jean Lazarus. You're pathetic, Colleen. You and Emma-Jean Lazarus. What a pair."

Laura made a gross snorting sound.

"You've really done it, Colleen," she said. "It's all over."

She spun around and walked out of the locker room.

Colleen had never in her life felt so alone.

But she was not alone.

There was a clang from the other end of the locker room, some footsteps, and the whoosh of a toilet flushing. A moment later Mr. Johannsen appeared, holding a bucket and plunger.

"Sorry," Mr. Johannsen said. "Toilet's on the fritz again."

Colleen nodded and tried to smile, but her face was numb.

Mr. Johannsen looked at her.

"Anything I can do for you, missy?"

Somehow, Colleen managed to stand up.

"Thank you, but I'm really fine," she said.

Mr. Johannsen stared at her. Colleen knew she must look completely hideous, but she guessed Mr. Johannsen didn't care about that.

"Okay, missy. You don't worry about it, then. You hear me?"

Colleen managed a little nod.

Mr. Johannsen left Colleen in the locker room.

It's hard to say how long it took for Colleen to make her way out of the locker room. Because Colleen wasn't really Colleen anymore. She was no longer exactly a person. She was like a zombie. Zombie Colleen. The real Colleen, terrified and small, was hiding inside zombie Colleen, who was large and had no fear or any other feelings.

Zombie Colleen carried real Colleen through the halls of William Gladstone Middle School and out the side door and all the way home. Her mom was waiting at the front door, looking furious.

"What took you so long!" she scolded. "I've been worried sick!"

"Mommy . . ."

"What is it? You don't look right!"

Of course Colleen didn't look right.

"Are you ill?" She put a cold hand to Colleen's forehead.

Yes, sick, very, very ill.

A zombie.

Chapter 19

Colleen Pomerantz was not in school the next day. Emma-Jean questioned Kaitlin Vogel about Colleen's whereabouts. "I talked to her last night and she sounded real bad," Kaitlin said. "Some stomach thing."

When Colleen still hadn't returned to school the next day, or the next, Emma-Jean grew concerned. Perhaps Colleen was not taking the proper palliative measures. For example, a person experiencing digestive problems should avoid all dairy products, which can cause irritation in the intestines and bowel. Emma-Jean believed it was prudent to personally communicate this information to both Colleen and her mother.

After school, Emma-Jean walked directly to Colleen's small brick house. In anticipation of the upcoming Easter holiday, the manicured evergreen bushes in front of the house were decorated with pink, yellow, and light-blue plastic eggs. Emma-Jean pressed the doorbell, which chimed loud and cheerful, as one would expect at Colleen's house. Emma-Jean expected to hear quick footsteps, and then see a pale but nonetheless smiling face through the windowed door. But the house remained silent, and nobody appeared. She rang again, and again. Emma-Jean sat down on the stoop. She would wait.

Fifteen minutes had passed when, sensing some movement behind her, Emma-Jean turned around and looked up at the house. There was Colleen, looking through a curtained upstairs window. Emma-Jean stood up and waved, but Colleen's face disappeared.

Emma-Jean went back to the door and pressed the bell, pleased this trip had not been in vain. Perhaps Colleen had been in the bathroom or shower when Emma-Jean had first rung the doorbell. Emma-Jean stood expectantly, certain that at any moment Colleen herself would open the door and invite her in.

Minutes passed, and Colleen did not open the door. Emma-Jean put her ear against the door. No sound was audible from inside the house.

This was most perplexing.

Emma-Jean backed away from the door and looked up at the curtained window through which Colleen had been peering. There was no sign of Colleen. In fact, to the casual observer, the house would appear completely empty.

However, Emma-Jean was not a casual observer. Colleen Pomerantz was in this house. And there was only one explanation for her failure to respond to the doorbell: She was too weak, perhaps in a state of collapse. Very likely, her mother had gone to the market or the drugstore, believing that Colleen's condition was stable. Perhaps she was unaware of the capricious nature of viruses, how symptoms can subside only to flare suddenly and violently just hours later.

Colleen could be helplessly writhing on the floor with agonizing cramps, delirious with fever. Ringing the doorbell wouldn't do. Emma-Jean needed to gain entry into the house. Immediately.

Emma-Jean pulled on the front door, which was locked. She ran to the garage doors, which were bolted closed. She ran all around the perimeter of the house, checking the side entrance and the rear sliding doors. All were locked.

Emma-Jean stood breathless in the front of the house. She studied a mature magnolia tree next to the front stoop. Its limbs reached up past the roof of the house. Several large branches led directly to the upstairs window.

It had been nearly two and a half years since Emma-Jean had climbed, but the motions came right back to her, as if they had been programmed into her limbs. She shimmied up the skinny trunk like her father had taught her, keeping her knees tight together. She grabbed the lowest branch, hoisting herself up in the manner of a gymnast mounting the uneven parallel bars. At several junctures, the branches formed sturdy V-shaped joints, providing footholds for Emma-Jean's white Keds. She was mindful not to disturb the tiny buds that were forming, and kept her feet clear of the most delicate branches.

Near the top, a thick branch led directly to the curtained window through which Emma-Jean had seen Colleen's face. Emma-Jean straddled the branch and crossed her feet at the ankles for stability. She leaned forward and peered through the window. She was relieved to see that Colleen was not sprawled on the floor, senseless with pain. She was sitting on her bed. Her shoulders were slumped and her hair looked unclean. Other than that, she did not look physically impaired in any way.

Emma-Jean rapped on the window until Colleen looked in her direction.

Chapter 20

Colleen had spent most of the past two days staring at her walls, which were painted a soft pastel pink. When Colleen had picked out the wall color last year, it had reminded her of everything she loved most in the world: candy hearts and strawberry ice cream and the cutest little piglets.

Now the color made her feel like she was trapped inside an old dog's ear. It made her sick, which is why she stared at it. She was glad to feel sick because then she didn't have to lie to her mother. So far it was working. Her parents and the doctor believed she had some mysterious virus.

"It's just not like Colleen," her mother had told

the doctor. "She's always so agreeable. Now we can't get her out of her room."

"Is anything going on at school?" the doctor said, wrinkling her large forehead in concern. "Is something upsetting you, Colleen?"

"No, of course not," her mother said. "Colleen is a straight-A student with dozens of friends."

The doctor had looked at Colleen in a really sweet way, and Colleen wanted so much to tell her. But zombie Colleen didn't go blabbing to nosy doctors.

The doctor had checked her throat and her ears. She pressed all around her stomach. "Can you tell me how you're feeling, Colleen?" she'd asked.

"It hurts," Colleen said. "Everywhere."

Colleen and her mother were sent to a lab, where a young man with a shaved head and soft rubber gloves had poked a needle into Colleen's arm and taken three vials of blood. Colleen had stared as the blood rushed through the skinny plastic tube into the glass vials. She wished the man would take all of her blood. Then she'd never have to go back to school. She'd never have to face Laura Gilroy again.

Colleen heard the knocking on her window and turned to see the pale face of Emma-Jean Lazarus staring at her from outside.

Now, officially, things could not get weirder.

Colleen had never hated anyone in her entire life. Not Laura Gilroy, who tried to steal her best friend. Not Brandon Mahoney, who had thrown a dead squirrel at her in kindergarten. And yet when she thought about Emma-Jean Lazarus, a sharp pain went through her stomach. She wasn't sure if it was hate. But it was something dark and very bad, something that Father William might warn against in one of his sermons.

Emma-Jean Lazarus had forged a letter on school stationery to Laura Gilroy.

Emma-Jean Lazarus had let Laura Gilroy find out.

Emma-Jean Lazarus had ruined Colleen's life.

But still, Colleen couldn't bring herself to let Emma-Jean sit outside in the freezing cold high up on that tree.

Slowly, Colleen rose from her bed. She padded

across the flowered rug, unlocked her window, and yanked it up so it was wide open. Emma-Jean climbed through the window. She brushed off her pants and rubbed her hands together.

"What are you doing here?" Colleen said in a raspy zombie voice.

"I came over to tell you that you should be avoiding dairy products," Emma-Jean said. "They are most irritating to the digestive tract and should be avoided by a person in your condition."

The normal Colleen would have smiled and nodded and pretended she knew exactly what Emma-Jean Lazarus was talking about. But Colleen wasn't normal.

"Look," zombie Colleen said. "You got me into big trouble. Laura Gilroy knows everything. She even has the note that I wrote you. She said you had it in a file in your room."

"How could she know that?"

"Has Laura Gilroy been to your room?"

"Yes," Emma-Jean said. "On Monday."

"Did you happen to notice if she stole something?"

"I don't think she would steal anything from my room," Emma-Jean said. Surely even Laura Gilroy wouldn't break the law.

"Of course she would! You have no idea, Emma-Jean! She has no morals at all! Were you with her the whole time?"

"She began to choke," Emma-Jean said. "And she requested something to drink."

"And?"

"I went downstairs to get her some grape juice."

"And she was alone in your room?"

"Yes."

"For how long?"

"Perhaps several minutes. I had no alternative. She was choking."

"No she wasn't! She wanted you to leave, so she could find some proof! She went into your desk and stole the file with my name on it. Why would you keep a file with my name on it!"

"I keep everything important in a file."

"I can't believe you did this, Emma-Jean! Why did you have to butt in? I didn't ask you to!"

"Yes you did," Emma-Jean said. "You said you wanted help."

"I didn't mean it! Why would I want help from YOU? Why are you even here?"

"I wanted to tell you to avoid dairy foods," Emma-Jean said. "I wanted to help you—"

"What are you talking about? Just go, Emma-Jean!" she wailed. "Just go away."

Emma-Jean didn't know what to do. Colleen was telling her to leave, and yet she was obviously in deep distress. Emma-Jean wanted to assist her, but Colleen didn't seem to want her help.

Colleen threw herself onto her bed with such force that the cat-shaped clock on her night table crashed to the floor, its eyes frozen open in a deathly stare.

Colleen was crying loudly now, sobbing, sputtering, and gasping. The sound made Emma-Jean's head ache. It was the worst sound Emma-Jean had ever heard. It was worse than slamming lockers or the screeching of car tires. This was the sound of misery. Of grief. Of things you couldn't control. Emma-Jean had heard a sound like this once before in her life. When her father died, Emma-Jean herself had made this sound.

Emma-Jean rushed toward the window, away from Colleen and her sobs.

"Emma-Jean!" Colleen called.

Emma-Jean stepped up to the windowsill and climbed out onto the magnolia tree.

"Emma-Jean, no!" Colleen shouted.

Emma-Jean started climbing down, but in her haste her foot slipped. She fell back into the cold air—down, down, down. And then she was lying in the cold dirt, staring up at the bright winter sky.

Chapter 21

Emma-Jean lay on her back, her head turned so that her left ear was pressed to the ground. There was an entire world in the dirt, filled with dramatic scenes of birth, survival, and often violent death. When she was younger, before she began her close studies of her fellow students, she had spent most of her time studying the natural world around her. She would lie in the grass, often for hours at a time, studying ants and worms and bees and beetles, the movement of the blades of grass in the wind, the shadows cast by the robins and jays and doves that flew overhead. Every moment was unique, Emma-Jean discovered, and captivating. And yet it was true that most people, including her sensible mother, paid no attention to the natural world around them.

Yet her father had paid attention. Often he had joined her in the grass, lying next to her, very still, alert. Emma-Jean tried to conjure the presence of her father next to her, the warmth of his shoulder touching hers, the feeling of their fingers intertwined, the sound of his voice whispering, his low, rumbling laugh. But she couldn't. Her father had slipped away from her.

"Emma-Jean! Are you okay? Oh gosh!"

Colleen Pomerantz.

Emma-Jean closed her eyes as Colleen knelt down next to her, so close that Emma-Jean felt warmed by Colleen's body. She felt Colleen's fingers softly brush against her hair. Colleen was sobbing still, but softer. "I'm so sorry!" she whispered. "I'm so sorry!"

A car pulled up. A door slammed and footsteps shook the ground.

"Oh my Lord! What's happened!" yelled a loud, shrill voice. "Colleen! Who is that?"

"Mommy!" Colleen screamed. "She fell out of the tree! It's Emma-Jean Lazarus! Emma-Jean Lazarus fell out of a tree!"

Chapter 22

Colleen wasn't a zombie anymore.

She wanted to be a zombie. Because it was way easier being zombie Colleen than being nice, normal Colleen. Zombie Colleen didn't care about anything or anyone. Nice, normal Colleen cared way too much about everything and everyone.

But it turned out that nice, normal Colleen was stronger than zombie Colleen. The sight of Emma-Jean Lazarus lying in the grass had caused nice, normal Colleen to leap out of zombie Colleen. There had been a showdown. Colleen had felt the two parts of her duking it out for control, like in a video game her mother wouldn't let her play. Nice, normal Colleen had kicked zombie Colleen's butt.

But now that Colleen was back to normal, she *really* couldn't stop crying. Even after Emma-Jean opened her eyes and sat up. Even after Colleen's mom helped Emma-Jean into the house. Even after Emma-Jean's mother came, and took Emma-Jean to the doctor, and called Colleen's mother to say Emma-Jean was okay.

Colleen just sobbed and sobbed.

And now that zombie Colleen was gone, Colleen couldn't lie to her mother anymore. She couldn't pretend to be sick. She told her mother everything, from the beginning: how Laura had tried to steal Kaitlin, how Emma-Jean had tried to help, even though Colleen hadn't asked her to, not on purpose anyway. Emma-Jean had gotten the wrong idea, and written this letter to Laura, and Laura had figured it all out and blamed Colleen, and then . . .

"I was so horrible!" Colleen wailed.

"It's okay," her mother kept saying. "Everything's fine now."

"No!" Colleen screamed. "It's not fine! I said so many horrible things to Emma-Jean! It will never be okay!"

"Please," her mother said. "You must calm down. It was an accident! Nobody is mad at you. Oh Colleen, why do you always take everything so hard?"

Colleen just shook her head.

"I don't know what to do for you," her mother said.

Colleen knew what her mother could do. Her mom could get up out of her chair and come close to Colleen. Her mom could kneel down on the floor and wipe away Colleen's tears with her bare hands, and kiss her right in the middle of the forehead. Her mom could hug her and whisper, "Colleen! I understand! I'm right here! I love you no matter what!"

Maybe then Colleen would stop crying.

But her mother wasn't the touchy, huggy, lovey type. She just wasn't.

Her mother did look worried. And once she patted Colleen's hand. But that wasn't enough. Colleen kept crying. She felt as if all the sadness she'd ever felt—all the sadness in the world—was pouring down her face.

Chapter 23

Emma-Jean and her mother had gone directly to the hospital. They waited for two hours for a doctor to examine Emma-Jean, and another hour for an X-ray to confirm what the doctor suspected: Emma-Jean had a cracked rib.

"You are a lucky person," said the young and competent doctor. He was about the same age as Vikram, and had a similarly soothing tone of voice. "A fall like that, I don't want to scare you, but I'd say you've got someone looking out for you."

Emma-Jean didn't tell the doctor or her mother what she almost remembered, and almost believed: that the branches of the magnolia tree had reached out to slow her fall. She recognized the absurdity of this notion, that she was likely feeling the clouding effects of the medication she'd been given for pain. But this dreamlike memory stayed with her, and she made no effort to clear it from her mind.

"I promise you'll heal quickly," the doctor said, looking Emma-Jean in the eye. "You'll be back to your old self in no time."

"Yes," Emma-Jean said, as this was exactly her intention: to return to her old self, the person she was before she met Colleen Pomerantz in the girls' room, before she developed the regrettable notion that she should get involved with her peers.

She had not solved Colleen's problem. On the contrary, she had created a new problem, a problem so large that it now seemed to occupy a separate universe, governed by mysterious laws and powerful forces. Emma-Jean couldn't begin to understand this problem. Even Poincaré, she suspected, would throw up his hands in confusion.

All Emma-Jean knew was this: Some irrational, emotional force had compelled her to enter the chaotic world of her peers, where the rules of logic did not apply.

She would not allow this to happen again. In fact, Emma-Jean decided then and there that she would not return to William Gladstone Middle School at all. She would resume her studies on her own, without the distraction of her peers and their problems.

Emma-Jean and her mother came home after eleven o'clock. The house was dark and silent and the floors creaked as they walked to the kitchen. Her mother helped Emma-Jean off with her coat and into a chair. Emma-Jean watched her mother prepare a can of tomato soup. Her mother seemed to intuit that Emma-Jean did not wish to further discuss the day's dramatic events. She had told her mother only the basic facts—that she had gone to Colleen's house after school, and she had fallen from the magnolia tree.

Her mother sat quietly while Emma-Jean ate her soup. She rose several times to get Emma-Jean a glass of juice, and to cut her up an apple, which

Emma-Jean did not touch. When Emma-Jean was ready, her mother led her up the stairs. "Should we go to my room?" her mother asked.

Emma-Jean shook her head. "I am very tired," she said.

Her mother helped her undress and kissed her good night. Emma-Jean got into bed and closed her eyes. Her chest throbbed and her legs ached and her mind felt dim, as though it had been drained of power. She closed her eyes and was nearly asleep when she suddenly sat up. She struggled to get out of bed. Moving very slowly, she stood up and walked to Henri's cage. The bird had been locked up all day. How could she have forgotten him?

She opened the cage door. In the darkness she could see only the outlines of Henri's tiny body as he hopped out and fluttered up onto her shoulder. Emma-Jean was too tired to whisper her usual greetings. She hoped Henri would understand. He leaned his head against her cheek. Emma-Jean stood very still. She reached up and lightly scratched Henri's neck. But she was so tired, and it hurt to stand. She went back to her bed and sat down. Henri fluttered up and settled on her headboard. He stood very straight, with his head up, like a sentry.

Emma-Jean lay down and closed her eyes.

It was not normal practice for Henri to spend the night outside of his cage. But this, after all, had not been a normal day.

It was past noon when Emma-Jean woke up. Henri was perched on her desk, regarding an exceptionally bright and sunny day out the window. Emma-Jean's mind was refreshed and filled immediately with scenes from the day before—Colleen's flowered carpet, the open window, the magnolia tree. With great effort, Emma-Jean pushed those images from her mind. No amount of thought would enable her to understand the sequence of missteps that led her into the cold dirt under the Pomerantzes' tree. And it made no sense to squander her intellectual energy on fruitless reflection.

She resolved to spend the day on some of the hobbies that she had neglected these past weeks. She was eager to resume her old routines.

Her mother, who had taken the day off from work, helped her dress and made her an egg for breakfast. She suggested that they go to a movie, or take a drive, but Emma-Jean declined. She went back up to her room, sat down at her desk, and looked out the window. She began reciting the names of all of the flora and fauna she could see. She started with just the trees: Bradford pear, possumshaw holly, river birch, dogwood, pine, ash. She recited the names out loud, followed by the Latin names—*pyrus callerana, ilex desidua, betula nigra, cornis florida . . .* Her mind started to drift. She thought of Colleen. She thought of Will Keeler, and what preparations he might be making for basketball camp. She thought of Vikram and his mother and the mango tree outside their home. She thought of Ms. Wright and the interesting insights she might have into the last chapters of *To Kill a Mockingbird.*

Emma-Jean redoubled her efforts to remain focused on the flora and fauna, but now she wondered about the point of this activity. It had been enjoyable when she and her father had stood in the yard together, reciting the names like a song, faster and faster, until one of them began to laugh.

But what was the point of reciting them over and over by herself?

She sat at her desk and took out her sketchpad, paging through the drawings she'd made over the years. There were detailed studies of many tree species, including some exotic varieties. Some of the drawings had taken days to complete, days on which Emma-Jean had been so engrossed that she had barely eaten or even looked up from the paper. Now her drawings failed to inspire her. She could not imagine picking up a pencil and applying it to the paper.

Worst of all was the sight of her father's dogwood tree, which had always filled her with calm. Now looking at it made her angry. Her heart began to race.

She did not want her father's tree. She did not

want her father's photographs or his books or his briefcase.

She wanted her father.

And right then it hit her, the most outlandish, illogical notion of all: that her father was gone from this world, and that Emma-Jean had been left behind to live without him.

Chapter 24

Colleen's mother had woken her up at 9:00 with a gentle pat on the head.

Colleen's eyes were so swollen, she could barely open them. Her pillow was damp.

"Can you get dressed right now?" her mother said. "I made you an English muffin that you can eat in the car."

"Where are we going?"

"To talk to someone."

Colleen figured they were going to see Emma-Jean, but she was wrong.

"No!" Colleen cried as they pulled into the parking lot of St. Mary's Church. "Not confession!"

"You're not going to confession," her mother said. "You're going to talk to Father William."

Colleen wailed. "I don't want him to know!"

"Colleen!" her mother said, unbuckling her seat belt. "Please! Father William can help you."

Colleen let her mother lead her through the church's carved metal door, and down a small, creaking staircase that led to the rectory. Mrs. White, the ninety-four-year-old church secretary, smiled and loudly told them to just have a seat. Colleen sat down on one of the metal chairs, but her mother did not.

"I want you to talk to him by yourself," she said.

Colleen grabbed her mother's wrist. "But . . ."

Her mother removed Colleen's hand, holding it for a second before letting go.

"It's better this way, Colleen." Her voice was gentle and her eyes were wide open. For the first time in her life Colleen realized that she and her mom had exactly the same hazel-colored eyes. "Talk to Father William, Colleen. Let him help you."

Her mom turned to leave, but then suddenly reached out and took Colleen by the shoulders and pulled her into her scratchy wool coat. "I'll be right in the car waiting, if you need me," she said, letting go and hurrying out the door.

Colleen almost ran out after her, but then she heard a door open.

"Colleen? How did you know I needed a little light in my day?" Father William stood smiling, his collar a little crooked, his thick gray hair not quite combed. Hanging from his neck were his reading glasses and also the carved wooden cross he'd gotten in Guatemala, where he'd been in the Peace Corps. At youth group meetings he'd take it off and let the kids try it on.

Colleen held back her tears until they had stepped into the small office and Father William had closed the door. Then, for the millionth time, she started to sob.

Father William did not try to stop her. He leaned close to her as she cried, patting her arm. Somehow, she sputtered out the whole story.

"And that's why Emma-Jean fell out of the tree," she said finally.

"But I understand from your mother that Emma-Jean is all right."

Colleen nodded.

"But here's the thing, what I've realized . . ." She took a deep, hiccupping breath. "I'm really not a good person, Father William. I try to be, but inside I'm really not." She gulped hard and came out with the rest. "I don't really care about other people. Mainly I think I care about myself."

She knew Father William would shake his head in disappointment, like he did during his sermons, when he spoke about people who were greedy and didn't care about the environment.

"I'm so, so sorry, Father William," she said, dropping her head, afraid to see the look on his face. Probably he would ask her to leave the youth group.

"Oh, it's a struggle, isn't it?" he said.

"What is?"

"To be kind. To do the right thing."

Here it comes, Colleen thought.

"We're all a little selfish, a little thoughtless and unkind," Father William went on. "I know I am."

"You?"

She looked at him. He did not look totally disappointed. He wasn't exactly smiling, but he wasn't not smiling either.

"Some days I'm a little tired, or impatient, and when someone comes to me with a problem, I don't give them the attention I should. I make them feel like their problem is silly."

"Really?" Colleen said.

Father William nodded. "And sometimes, when that good woman Mrs. White doesn't wear her hearing aid, and she can't hear one thing I say, or the phone ringing, or that someone's knocking on the door, I get impatient with her."

Colleen nodded. Mrs. White was so sweet. She hoped Father William never made Mrs. White feel embarrassed about being practically deaf.

"But here's what happens to me. Can I tell you?"

Colleen nodded.

"I realize I've behaved in a shabby way, and I feel lousy about it. I sit here, right in this chair, and think to myself, well, Bill, you blew it!"

Colleen watched Father William closely. Her bangs were limp and soggy from all her crying, so she pushed them back.

"I remember that I can make things right again. I call that person with the little problem. And I say, gee, Max—I'll call him Max—I was thinking about your problem, and I'd like to talk about it a little more. And we have a good talk and by the time we're ready to hang up, I can tell he feels better."

Colleen was sure that person felt better after talking to Father William, just like Colleen was starting to feel better now.

"And when I've been a little short with Mrs. White, I sneak out and buy her some chocolates. And not the cheap kind. She loves those samplers, with the soft centers. Do you like those?"

"I love those!"

"Me too," Father William said, taking a sip of water from the tall glass on his desk.

Father William took the box of tissues from his bookshelf and held it out to Colleen. She took one and gave her nose a good blow.

"I will apologize to Emma-Jean," Colleen said, wiping her nose. "I mean, I already did, but I'll make it up to her."

"I'm sure you will."

Colleen would! She would invite Emma-Jean over and they would make popcorn balls or bead necklaces or . . . they could sit and look at trees, if that's what Emma-Jean wanted to do. Who knew? Maybe that was really fun! And Colleen would tell Kaitlin and Valerie and Michele how Emma-Jean had tried to help her, and that once they got to know Emma-Jean they'd see that she wasn't so weird, not really, and even if she was a little weird, she was such a good person, it didn't matter.

Colleen's mother was so smart to have brought her to talk to Father William!

"I've known you your whole life, haven't I?" Father William said.

Of course he had. He had baptized Colleen when she was just a few weeks old.

"And I'm looking at you now, and I can tell you, with great authority, that you are a very fine human being."

"Really?" Colleen said. She tried not to smile, but she couldn't stop herself. "It is so nice of you to say that."

"Just promise me one thing?" Father William said.

"Anything!" she said.

"Never stop struggling!" he said in a sharp voice, smiling and giving his hands one sharp clap and stamping his foot.

"I won't!" Colleen said, giving her own hands a clap in return.

Mrs. White opened the door. "Yes Father, you needed me?"

Father William and Colleen looked at each other, but of course Colleen didn't laugh.

Father William stood up. "Mrs. White, I always need you! What would you say if I asked you to let Colleen and me sample a couple of those chocolates I gave you yesterday?"

Chapter 25

The following afternoon, Emma-Jean was cleaning out Henri's cage when out of her bedroom window, she saw something extraordinary: Colleen Pomerantz, followed by Kaitlin Vogel, Valerie Rosen, and Michele Peters. The procession of girls marched up her brick walk and onto the porch. The doorbell rang, and Emma-Jean heard the squeak of the front door, followed by a chorus of high-pitched voices.

Moments later her mother appeared at her bedroom door.

"Emma-Jean. There are some girls here to see you, some friends of yours from school."

"They are not my friends," Emma-Jean informed her mother.

"They said they were."

"What did they say exactly?"

"They said, 'Hello, we're friends of Emma-Jean's. We missed her and wanted to see if she's feeling better.'"

"They said that?"

"Yes."

"Are you certain that is all they said?"

"Yes. And they brought you some cookies, and some of your homework from school."

"That will not be necessary because I am not planning to return to William Gladstone."

"What? Emma-Jean, of course you are! You're going to feel much better over the next few days."

Emma-Jean knew she needed to explain her plan to her mother, but now was not the appropriate time.

"Come!" her mother said, taking Emma-Jean's hand. "We can't keep those girls waiting. It's very rude!"

Emma-Jean held her mother's hand as they walked down the stairs into the waiting cluster of girls. Her mother let go as the girls encircled Emma-Jean.

"We just wanted to stop by for a minute to see if you were okay!" Colleen said.

"Yeah!" said Valerie.

"That's right," said Kaitlin. "Everyone misses you!"

"Everyone!" said Michele.

The girls huddled closer around her.

"I hope you're better by Friday," said Colleen. "For the leprechaun dance."

Emma-Jean recalled the posters taped to the walls of the William Gladstone lobby, advertising the special event in celebration of St. Patrick's Day. There would be music and dancing, food and drink. Emma-Jean had not considered buying a ticket. She imagined that the cafeteria would be crowded and loud and overheated.

"We were thinking we could all go together," Colleen said.

"Yeah," said Valerie.

"That's right," said Kaitlin.

"Together," said Michele.

It took Emma-Jean a long moment to realize that "together" included her.

Emma-Jean opened her mouth to say no, but shut it quickly when, quite surprisingly, she nearly said the word *yes*.

Did she want to go to the dance?

No, of course she did not.

"No, thank you," she said, righting herself. "I won't be at the dance."

"Why not?" said Colleen.

"Yeah," said Valerie.

"Come on!" said Kaitlin.

"You have to come!" said Michele.

"I am sorry," Emma-Jean said.

The girls looked at one another. They exchanged shrugs and raised eyebrows and soft sighs. And then Colleen suggested that maybe they should be going.

"You're probably really worn out from everything," Colleen said. "I mean you don't look worn out, you look gorgeous, as usual! It's just that you need to rest, so that you can change your mind and come to the dance! With us!"

"Yeah!" said Valerie.

"That's right," said Kaitlin.

"With us!" said Michele.

Emma-Jean thanked them for the cookies.

The girls said good-bye and departed in a flurry of pastel parkas and freshly painted nails. Their fruity, flowery smells lingered in the hallway.

Emma-Jean felt odd, like she had just returned from a long trip.

Her mother was standing in the kitchen doorway, waiting for her.

They sat down at the kitchen table.

"They seem like lovely girls," said her mother.

"Yes," said Emma-Jean.

"Don't you think they would be disappointed if you didn't return to school?"

Emma-Jean considered this.

"No," she said. "They will not miss me. Until a few weeks ago, I hardly spoke to them at all."

"But how about now? They said you were friends."

Emma-Jean shook her head. "They are too complicated."

Her mother shook her head and smiled, an odd reaction, Emma-Jean thought.

"I'm sorry, Emma-Jean!" her mother said. It took a moment for the smile to fade from her face. "I'm smiling because your father used to say the exact same thing."

"He did?"

Emma-Jean eyed her father's picture on the refrigerator.

"Yes. You know, this all didn't come naturally to him, connecting with other people. He had to work at it. And then, oh Emma-Jean, when you came into the world, we were so madly in love with you! He wanted to show you everything! I think in so many ways you were the one who pulled him into the world. Because it became so much easier for him. You remember how much he enjoyed his students? And how they loved him!"

Emma-Jean remembered the students—hundreds of them—who had come to her father's memorial service, young men and women who leaned against each other and cried, who stood in line to tell Emma-Jean and her mother how much her father had encouraged and inspired them.

"Emma-Jean," her mother said softly. "It was good of you to try to help Colleen when you saw her crying in the bathroom."

"How do you know about that?"

"Mrs. Pomerantz called," she said. "She's called four times. She told me . . . it's quite a story."

"Did she tell you about the letter I wrote?"

Emma-Jean's mother nodded. "Yes, and for future reference, forging letters isn't a good idea, even for noble purposes."

"I accomplished nothing. I made Colleen very unhappy. I made her problem much worse."

Her mother leaned close to Emma-Jean so their noses almost touched.

"Listen closely to me."

"I always listen closely to you."

Her mother smiled and put her hands on Emma-Jean's. "Things don't always work out the way we want them to. We try, and sometimes we get hurt, and sometimes we cry. I guess you could say we even fall out of a tree, in a manner of speaking. But we get up. And next time we don't go up the same tree, or maybe we go up, but hold on tighter."

Emma-Jean's mother stood up and carefully took her father's picture off the refrigerator. She knelt down next to Emma-Jean and handed her the picture. Her father seemed to regard them both with love and care.

"Do you know what your father's favorite quote was? It was by Poincaré, of course." Emma-Jean's mother brushed the hair from Emma-Jean's face and leaned close to her ear. *"It is by logic that we prove, but it is in our hearts that we discover life's possibilities."*

Emma-Jean found it perplexing that she'd never read that statement. Maybe she really didn't know Poincaré at all.

"I'm not like other people," Emma-Jean said.

"Yes you are," her mother said. "More than you know." She wiped away some of the tears that were running down Emma-Jean's face. "Maybe it's time you accepted it."

Chapter 26

The William Gladstone Middle School cafeteria looked so amazing, with all the green Christmas lights and sparkly green and white streamers and shamrocks hanging from the ceiling. Colleen herself had helped paint the big sign on the wall that said: "Welcome to the Leprechaun Dance!" The L and the D were crooked, but Colleen guessed it didn't look too bad and that not too many people noticed.

The tables and chairs had been folded up and pushed against the wall to make room for a dance floor. Michele, Valerie, and Kaitlin were right in the middle, lined up doing some dance steps. They kept stopping and cracking up, and Colleen wished she could be with them.

But right now she was working up her nerve to talk to Laura Gilroy.

The past two days she'd avoided Laura in school, rushing out of Spanish right when the bell rang, going to extra math help during lunch, sneaking into the teachers' bathroom when she absolutely had to go. She kept expecting Laura to corner her, to wave the stolen file in her face or drag her into Mr. Tucci's office. But Laura barely looked at her. Was this some new form of slow torture?

It didn't matter, really, because now Colleen was going to make things right. She didn't want to be afraid anymore. If she was afraid, then zombie Colleen might be able to sneak back into her life. She couldn't let that happen. She had to face up to Laura, who would be horrible and mean. But Colleen would just have to take it.

Colleen gathered up her nerve and made her way through the crowds of seventh graders, sweaty in their green T-shirts and hats. Laura was standing at the edge of the dance floor, swaying to the music. She was staring at Will Keeler, who was with his friends, jumping up and trying to pull the shamrocks from the ceiling. Laura's eyes were all dreamy. In better times, Laura had confided in Colleen that she and Will Keeler were meant to be together. She'd told Colleen about her plan to make things official tonight, at the dance. "Won't we make the most perfect couple?" Laura had said.

"Yes!" Colleen had said, even though she wasn't exactly sure Will Keeler liked Laura. Will Keeler was really cute, but he seemed more interested in basketball than in girls.

Colleen stepped up, took a deep breath, and tapped Laura on the shoulder.

Laura whipped around. "What?"

"Laura," she said, "I wanted to say sorry for all that happened . . ."

Laura looked at her in her mean way, like Colleen was a fly on Laura's salad. But Colleen didn't back away.

"Things got a little out of control, and . . ." Colleen

paused because her heart was beating like crazy and it was hard to breathe.

"What?" Laura said.

"And I know you're upset. But Emma-Jean didn't really understand. And when you meet with Mr. Tucci, and show him the file, you should maybe explain that. Or I will."

Laura rolled her eyes and laughed, like Colleen herself was the stupidest joke she'd ever heard.

"Guess what, Colleen. You guys got real lucky. Because there was a leak. A pipe burst over my locker, and everything got wrecked. Including the file."

"A leak?"

"That's right. That load Johannsen was trying to fix a pipe, and he botched it. Like a million gallons of water poured into my locker."

"Oh my gosh! That's awful."

"I'm over it, okay? I never really wanted to go on the ski trip. I heard that Kaitlin's condo's a real dump, anyway. And Emma-Jean Lazarus is a big ole freak. She's hopeless."

"But . . ."

Laura waved her hand at Colleen. "I'm sick of the whole thing. So let's just say it's over, okay? Done." She brushed her hands together like she was brushing away dirt. "We're friends again."

She looked back over at Will Keeler.

"You're sure?" Colleen said, trying to smile.

Laura waved her hand again. "Yeah."

"Well, great! So I guess we'll talk later, okay?"

"Yeah," Laura said without looking at her.

Colleen started to walk away. She had done it! Everything was okay! Now things could go back to normal, the way they were, before that morning when she met Emma-Jean Lazarus in the bathroom.

Colleen stopped short, her sneakers squeaking on the tile floor.

Wait! The way things were before? When Colleen cared too much about everything? When she was always afraid of making someone mad, or doing something wrong?

Is that what she wanted?

Before she could answer herself, she had rushed

back over to Laura. Colleen wasn't thinking. There was something controlling her, not the zombie. Something brand-new, good and strong. Something brave.

"No!" she said to Laura.

"Excuse me?"

"I take it back," Colleen said. "I'm not sorry about what happened."

"What is with you?" Laura snapped.

For a moment Colleen lost her nerve. What was she doing? Where was Kaitlin?

But then something amazing happened. Before her eyes, Laura Gilroy turned into a chimp. Colleen stared. Then she leaned right into Laura's personal space so Laura had to take a step back. Colleen stuck out her chest and bared her braces, just a little.

"You did a mean thing!" she said, softly at first. But then her voice got stronger. "You tricked Kaitlin into inviting you skiing. You knew it would hurt me!"

Laura Gilroy seemed to shrink, and Colleen felt herself getting bigger.

"You're . . ." Colleen fumbled for the right words, searching for the perfect thing to say. "You are not nice!"

Oh gosh! Had she really done that?

Colleen hurried away, her heart thumping, leaving Laura with her mouth hanging open.

Who was the alpha chimp now?

Chapter 27

Earlier that day, Emma-Jean had awakened just after dawn to the smell of curried eggs. With great haste, wincing from the pain in her rib, she put on her robe and slippers, unlocked Henri's cage, and ran down the stairs so fast that her bird had to dig his claws into her shoulder to keep from falling.

A familiar leather suitcase and Pittsburgh Steelers duffel stood in the hallway.

And in the kitchen, bent over the stove, was Vikram Adwani.

Emma-Jean had a great many questions to ask him, about his mother's health, about his trip home, and his future plans. These questions and others were arrayed in her mind. Emma-Jean opened her mouth to talk but then Vikram turned around and their eyes met and he very gently put his arms around Emma-Jean. She pressed her cheek against his heart.

Her questions vanished from her mind.

"I fell out of a tree," Emma-Jean said when they finally parted.

"I know. Your mother called me."

"She did?"

"Yes."

"How is your mother? Is she recovered?"

"Yes," Vikram said. "In fact, it was my mother who urged me to return. She was most concerned about you."

"Oh," Emma-Jean said.

Of course Emma-Jean had not forgotten the letter she had sent to Vikram's mother. She was suddenly struck by a most fantastic hope that the letter had gotten lost on its journey across two oceans and the vast African continent. She pictured it tossing in the waves of the Arabian Sea, the address rendered illegible by the salt water.

"My mother has expressed a strong interest in meeting you and is planning to visit in June," Vikram said, looking at Emma-Jean most intently, as if he were trying to decipher the fine print on an important document. "She says to tell you that you and she have much to discuss."

"Yes . . . well . . ." Emma-Jean said. "She knows of my interest in India."

"Of course," Vikram said. "Perhaps that's what she wishes to talk about."

"Of course," Emma-Jean said, with less than perfect certainty.

"She sent something for you," he said, hurrying into the hallway and returning a moment later with a bundle wrapped in many layers of tissue paper. He handed it to Emma-Jean. "She hopes very much that you are pleased with this. We worked on it night and day."

At that moment Emma-Jean's mother came into the kitchen, saw Vikram, and exclaimed, "Your flight arrived early!"

Vikram smiled and her mother's face lit up with

an expression as bright and pure as the sunlight streaming through the kitchen window. Her mother began questioning Vikram about the details of his mother's recovery. Emma-Jean took her package and slipped out of the kitchen, Henri fluttering after her.

She went upstairs and sat on her bed, ignoring the pain in her rib. Carefully, she unwrapped her gift, slowly peeling away the many layers of tissue paper.

It was her quilt. Emma-Jean shook it open, and stared in shock.

All around the edges of the quilt, the frayed and unraveled squares had been removed. In their place were squares of brightly colored sari silk, dozens of different colors, sewn together with tiny, even stitches. The new squares looked nothing like the old ones. They did not in any way fit the pattern her father had created.

And yet the effect was striking, a ribbon of jewels.

Emma-Jean hesitated a moment, and then slowly,

carefully, she wrapped the quilt around her shoulders. And there it was, the old feeling of comfort.

Emma-Jean leaned back on her bed. She could hear the clanging of pots downstairs and Vikram's low voice. Her mother's tinkling laugh floated up the stairs along with the smell of frying garlic and curry.

And then Emma-Jean sensed something else, an unfamiliar feeling, a kind of effervescence rising from somewhere deep inside her. It was as if some of the dazzling brightness of the quilt's new squares was flowing through her veins.

She sat very still, wondering what the feeling was, hoping that it would not subside.

Henri flew over and landed on her shoulder. She leaned her cheek against his.

Emma-Jean hugged the quilt tighter.

She looked up at her father's picture hanging on her wall, which smiled out at her, his green eyes bright. They regarded each other for some time, and then her father seemed to give Emma-Jean a reassuring nod.

Emma-Jean nodded back.

That evening, Vikram, Emma-Jean's mother, and Emma-Jean headed out for the movies. They drove in Vikram's car. It was a dark, moonless night, but up the road, William Gladstone Middle School was fully illuminated.

Of course, Emma-Jean remembered. The dance. She thought of the loud music and the salty snacks served in unhygienic communal bowls. She thought of her fellow seventh graders, how they would scream and shout and grow hoarse, how the music would pulsate against her eardrums. The floor would be sticky from spilled soda. The air would be stuffy and hot. Someone could bump into her, causing further injury to her rib.

"Vikram," she said. "Could you please pull into the school parking lot? I would like you to drop me off at my school."

Chapter 28

Emma-Jean lingered in front of the school after Vikram's car pulled slowly away. It was obvious, even from outside, that the cafeteria was very warm, as the windows were fogged. The music and shouts of her classmates, muffled only slightly by the walls of the school, rose up around her. She turned around and looked back out toward the street. The walk home would be pleasantly brisk on the dark and quiet streets, under the protective shadow of the elm trees and the watchful gazes of the nocturnal creatures. She could be home within ten minutes, cozy in her room, enjoying the quiet companionship of Henri.

And yet something propelled her forward, through

the front door of the school, and into the lobby. The door slammed behind her, as though an invisible hand had pushed it.

And then . . .

"Oh my gosh! You're here!!" shrieked Colleen Pomerantz, who came running toward her, dressed in head-to-toe kelly green. Kaitlin, Valerie, and Michele followed Colleen like emerald shadows.

"This is so amazing, I don't know what to say!" said Colleen, breathless. "I had a feeling you'd come! Didn't I? Didn't I say she would be here?"

"You did!" said Kaitlin.

"Amazing!" said Michele.

"How did you know?" said Valerie.

"Well, come on!" Colleen said, grabbing Emma-Jean's hand like she often grabbed the hands of Kaitlin or Valerie or Michele in the hall between classes. A sharp pain shot through Emma-Jean's rib as Colleen pulled her toward the cafeteria. She held her breath but did not let go of Colleen's hand.

"So are you ready to dance?" Colleen said, with a wiggle of her hips.

It was hard to hear over the pulsating music, so Emma-Jean had to shout "No!" several times and shake her head emphatically as the girls persisted in their pleas for Emma-Jean to join them on the crowded dance floor.

"Okay!" Colleen said "But you have to know, Emma-Jean, one day we'll get you out there. You know we will!"

She sounded so certain that Emma-Jean could almost picture herself standing alongside Colleen and her friends, kicking her legs high into the air and shaking her shoulders and gyrating her hips. The image was most amusing, and Emma-Jean laughed. The sound, not unlike her mother's laugh, seemed to startle Colleen and her friends, who regarded her with wide eyes.

It surprised Emma-Jean as well.

She conjured up the dancing image again, and once more she laughed.

The other girls laughed too.

"You're sure you don't want to?" Colleen said.

"Quite sure," Emma-Jean said.

Colleen and the other girls peeled away from Emma-Jean. They skipped together over to the dance floor and disappeared in the sea of bobbing heads and waving arms. Emma-Jean was satisfied to see her fellow seventh graders in such high spirits. Colleen, in particular, seemed restored to her usual state of cheer.

As Emma-Jean had predicted, the cafeteria was unpleasantly hot, and the music was irritating to Emma-Jean's sensitive ears. There were several teachers milling about, including Ms. Wright, who was elegantly dressed in a green dress that skimmed her ankles. When she saw Emma-Jean she smiled and waved, and Emma-Jean waved back. It was unfortunate for Ms. Wright that Vikram was no longer available to be her husband. However, it occurred to Emma-Jean that a woman as intelligent and attractive as Ms. Wright must have many suitors, and that Ms. Wright would have the good judgment to choose a man worthy of her. It also occurred to Emma-Jean that she could still invite Ms. Wright home for dinner, that her favorite teacher would fit in very well at their dining room table. She would extend the invitation first thing on Monday.

Despite the presence of Ms. Wright and other chaperones, some of the boys were engaged in questionable displays of revelry. Most alarmingly, Brandon Mahoney was tossing a full, two-liter bottle of Sprite high into the air. It spun on its way up and down, and Brandon caught it as though it were a football. He continued with this game, tossing the bottle higher and higher, harder and harder, to the encouraging hoots of his friends. And then, as was inevitable, Brandon failed to catch the bottle and it crashed to the floor. The bottle burst open, spewing a fizzing spray of liquid directly into his face, and also across the floor.

"Oh jeez!" Brandon cried.

Emma-Jean found Mr. Johannsen standing at the large, rusty sink, filling a large plastic bucket with water.

"Hello, missy," he said, smiling.

"Hello, Mr. Johannsen."

"Enjoying yourself?"

"It is very loud and too hot. There is a spill near the dance floor. I can show you where."

"I'm on the case," he said. "You don't worry about it. Go have some fun."

Emma-Jean watched as Mr. Johannsen lifted the bucket and, without spilling a drop, placed it on a small rolling cart. He took his mop from the corner and set the wooden handle on his shoulder like a musket.

"So I'm retiring at the end of this year," he said. "You know that, right?"

"No, I did not," Emma-Jean said, frowning.

"Thirty-four years," he said. "My wife and I have a little lake house, we'll see the grandkids more. It'll be nice and quiet."

"I'm pleased for you, but I am concerned that the facility will deteriorate after you are gone."

"They'll find someone to take my place. And you'll watch over things for me, help the new guy learn his way around, won't you?"

"Yes," she said. "Of course I will be here."

"Good. Now you hurry along. You have nothing to worry about. Nobody's going to cause you any trouble, not so long as I'm here."

Then Mr. Johannsen did something perplexing. He picked up a large wrench from the counter, held it in the air, and winked at her.

In the final minutes of the dance, Emma-Jean was in the girls' room. She was about to flush when someone entered the stall next to her. She peered underneath the wall: black, uncomfortable-looking high-heeled boots, green velvet pants.

Laura Gilroy.

Emma-Jean waited until Laura had flushed. She watched through the gap in the door as Laura stood at the mirror, combed her fingers through her hair, and smiled at her reflection. Emma-Jean was not the least bit surprised that Laura Gilroy did not wash her hands.

Emma-Jean was leaving the girls' room, her own hands well scrubbed, when she saw Laura Gilroy and Will Keeler talking in the corner of the hallway. She stopped and listened, concealing herself in the water fountain alcove.

"I gave you those chocolates, you know," Laura said.

"Oh. Thanks."

"So you have to dance with me!" Laura was saying. "I've been waiting all night. The dance is almost over."

"I told you," Will said, backing away. "I don't dance."

"Not even with me?"

"Nope."

"But that's not very nice," Laura said in a high, babyish voice. She put both hands on Will Keeler's shoulders.

Will broke away. "Gotta go!"

Laura Gilroy watched Will Keeler run back toward the cafeteria. And Emma-Jean watched Laura Gilroy.

Laura leaned her back against the pale yellow wall and slowly sank to the floor in the manner of a helium balloon with a leak. She closed her eyes and rested her forehead on her green velvet knees.

Laura Gilroy appeared so dejected that Emma-Jean considered offering some assistance. Emma-Jean was fairly certain that she could compel Will Keeler to dance with Laura. She had not forgotten what Will had said to her upon the successful resolution of his problem: that he owed her. Though Emma-Jean had not planned to accept his offer, she knew he was honorable, and would make good on his promise. If Emma-Jean asked him to dance with Laura Gilroy, he would do it. And Laura Gilroy would never have to know that Emma-Jean had intervened.

But Emma-Jean dismissed this idea. She was no longer interested in solving other people's problems. At least for now. And besides, it was possible that Will Keeler's favor would come in handy. Perhaps sometime in the not-so-distant future, Emma-Jean would want to dance with Will Keeler herself.

ACKNOWLEGMENTS: One page is not enough to express my gratitude to all of the people who helped and inspired me as I wrote this book. I would like to write a whole book of thank-yous for Nancy Mercado, my editor, who taught me so much, who took such great care with this book and with me. I am grateful to the entire Dial team, especially to Jessica Dandino, who helped edit this book; Regina Castillo, for her keen copyediting talents; Lauri Hornik, for her ideas and support; Kristen Smith for the beautiful cover and illustrations; and Teresa Kietlinski for creating such a lovely interior.

Another thick book of gratitude is for my agent Gail Hochman, who so graciously read my work years ago and gave me the confidence to keep trying.

Chaya Deitsch, Caroline Sherman, and Mary-Lou Weisman read an early draft of this book and urged me to keep with it. Without these fabulous women and their critical input through several drafts, this book would not exist.

Freja Andrews was ten years old when she became my first reader. Her kind words couldn't have meant more to me. My many friends and colleagues at *Storyworks* magazine helped me fall in love with the world of middle grade literature, and I especially thank David Goddy for giving me my start there.

I owe a heartfelt thank you to my family and friends who encouraged me along the way, in particular Karen and Barry Tarshis, Stefanie Dreyfuss, Deborah Dinger, Lynn Massey, Della Herden, Debbie Bofinger, and Michele Rubin, who offered ongoing help and encouragement over many years.

To my husband David, for this and everything, I am inexpressibly grateful.

Literature Circle Questions

Use these questions and the activities that follow to get more out of the experience of reading *Emma-Jean Lazarus Fell Out of a Tree* by Lauren Tarshis.

1. Who does Mr. Petrowski blame for his missing candy? Why?

2. What does Emma-Jean realize as her mother is saying good-bye to Vikram Adwani at the airport?

3. What happens that prevents Laura Gilroy from showing Mr. Tucci the file of evidence? Who is responsible?

4. Emma-Jean tries her best to help the people around her by channeling French mathematician Jules Henri Poincaré, who believed that "even the most complex problems could be solved through a process of creative thinking" (p. 9). Outline the problems Emma-Jean tackles in the book and summarize her solution to each.

5. Colleen tells Kaitlin that Emma-Jean is "just different"—and Emma-Jean herself would agree. Compare and contrast Emma-Jean and Colleen. How do the two girls view their peers? How do they handle problems?

6. At several points in the book, Emma-Jean has trouble understanding what others say and do. Choose a situation or comment she finds confusing. Then interpret the situation accurately and explain how Emma-Jean misunderstood.

7. On page 176, Emma-Jean's mother tells her about her father's favorite quote by Poincaré: *"It is by logic that we prove, but it is in our hearts that we discover life's possibilities."* How can this idea be applied to Emma-Jean's experiences?

8. Emma-Jean tries to make Colleen feel better by comparing Laura Gilroy with alpha chimpanzees, who "bare their teeth and beat their chests and achieve control of the group because the others feel threatened" (p. 89). Using specific examples from the text, show how Laura's behavior is similar to that of an alpha chimp.

9. The encounter between Emma-Jean and Colleen in the bathroom is a turning point for both girls. Compare the girls' thoughts and actions in chapters 1 and 2 with their thoughts and actions during the Leprechaun Dance. How have Emma-Jean and Colleen changed? Use quotations from the text to support your answer.

10. At the beginning of the book, Emma-Jean knows the quilt her father made needs to be repaired but can't find fabrics to fit with her father's intricate pattern. When she sees how Vikram Adwani's mother has fixed the quilt with colorful mismatched squares, Emma-Jean finds that "the effect was striking, a ribbon of jewels" (p. 188). Analyze Emma-Jean's appreciation of the repaired quilt. How does it demonstrate the ways in which she has changed?

11. When Vikram Adwani returns from his trip to India, he says his mother plans to visit and that she has "much to discuss" with Emma-Jean. What do you think Mrs. Adwani and Emma-Jean would say to each other? Write a short script of a possible conversation between them.

12. Emma-Jean doesn't take Laura Gilroy's feelings into consideration when she formulates her plan to help Colleen. Imagine that Laura kept a diary in which she recorded how she felt when she arrived at the school for the "rehearsal" and in the days afterward. Compose a series of diary entries in Laura's voice.

13. Emma-Jean's mother tells her that "for future reference, forging letters isn't a good idea, even for noble purposes" (p. 175). In your view, was Emma-Jean wrong to forge the letters? Why or why not?

14. Emma-Jean's mother says she thinks Will Keeler was defending her honor during the incident in the cafeteria and compares him to a knight. Do you think Will Keeler deserves this comparison? Use details from the text to support your answer.

15. Why do you think the author chose to title the book *Emma-Jean Lazarus Fell Out of a Tree*? In your opinion, is this a fitting title? Why or why not? Justify your answer using details from the book.

Note: These questions are keyed to Bloom's Taxonomy as follows: Knowledge: 1–3; Comprehension: 4–6; Application: 7–8; Analysis: 9–10; Synthesis: 11–12; Evaluation: 13–15.

Activities

1. Emma-Jean's father's hero was French mathematician and physicist Jules Henri Poincaré. Do some research about Poincaré's life and work. Then write a report or prepare a presentation for your class to share what you have learned.

2. William Gladstone Middle School is full of interesting characters. Create several pages of a school yearbook depicting the teachers and students in the novel. Sketch school portraits of the important characters and write captions describing each.

3. Emma-Jean and her mother love Vikram Adwani's cooking. Use cookbooks or the Internet to learn more about Indian cuisine. Then create your own guide to the foods mentioned in the book— chana masala, dal, paneer, korma, basmati rice, curried chicken and lentils, puran poli, chutney, chai tea, curried eggs—and other typical Indian dishes you discover. Include illustrations, descriptions, and recipes for each.

Author Web Site: http://www.laurentarshis.com